The Orphan Creed

by

Davitch Faryn Vago

authorHOUSE®

AuthorHouse™
1663 Liberty Drive
Bloomington, IN 47403
www.authorhouse.com
Phone: 1-800-839-8640

Published by AuthorHouse 12/9/2011

ISBN: 978-1-4567-6455-5 (sc)
ISBN: 978-1-4567-6453-1 (dj)
ISBN: 978-1-4567-6454-8 (e)

Library of Congress Control Number: 2011906967

"Standing in the ocean with the sun burning low in the west. Like a fire in the cavernous darkness at the heart of the beast. With my beliefs and possessions stopped at the frontier in my chest. At the edge of my country, my back to the sea, looking east.

Where the search for the truth is conducted with a wink and a nod. And where power and position are equated with the Grace of God. These times are famine for the soul while for the sense's, it's a feast. From the edge of my country, as far as you see, looking east."

Jackson Brown, Looking East.

To each of them who've loved me.
To those who've known me true.
To the Heaven that smiles above.
And waits my coming too.
To the cause that needs assistance.
To the wrongs that need resistance.
To the future in my distance.
And all the good that I can do.

Davitch Faryn Vago

Onward

The boy child lay unconscious and naked in the wet sand; rocked and cradled by the relentless gentle surf which lifted and dropped his body in the hypnotic rise and fall of each rolling cresting ripple of the lagoon.

He was badly burned by the subtropical sun. His skin was a brilliant, cherry red. His skin had the hue of a lobster that had been eased silently screaming into a pot of boiling water; only to emerge a few moments later a crimson lifeless thing.

The sun had danced merrily for many hours upon his silent, exposed form while he was basted alive by the fine, salty brine. Dozens of brittle epidermal splits had opened and coursed across the width and breadth of his neck, back, and legs like thick lines of demarcation on some macabre treasure map.

He was alone. He was dying.

The beach of the lagoon on which he lay was unremarkable except for the singular fact that it was deserted of all life. The fine white sand was smooth and bare of any of the detritus the ocean leaves as witness to the march of time in the tropics.

A coral reef line rose and fell a dull, pounding white in the surf several hundred yards from the opening into the lagoon.

A line of aging palm trees swayed in the warm ocean breeze marking a thick, forbidding border to the beach.

The sky was a mirror of the sea. Cloudless. Shining. Blue.

A full day passed, and half a night again before he finally stirred.

It was the cool of the night breeze and a violent shivering that slowly brought him back; if only for a few delirious moments; to a strange and unfamiliar world.

In those few semiconscious thoughts mixed brightly with his pain; he thought he could hear the echoes of rifle shots. In his childish delirium and his violent shaking; he thought he could hear voices.

Perhaps; he reasoned; it was the voice of angels or demons come to take him.

His sand-covered lips were cracked and split. His eyes fluttered wildly beneath their sand caked lids and he opened them briefly and then closed them just as quickly again. Somewhere in his dying mind; he thought he could see his mother's beautiful blue eyes.

His mouth worked to speak, but only a hoarse whisper escaped.

"Help me. Please God. Help me. Please." And then he was silent. He was gone deeper. Perhaps too deep for us to retrieve.

So soft was his plea; so tremulous and weak was his prayer; that only the fine white sand which nestled his mottled face rustled ever so slightly to acknowledge it.

As he shivered violently in the wet sand, he drifted backwards.

Backwards to the rifle shots. Back to the sounds of laughter. Falling.

As he fell; a strange warmth enveloped him.

He could feel a hand upon his face which seemed to be gently brushing the fine sand away. A woman's hand; soft. Warm. In the touch; he felt something he dimly remembered. Something kind. Something old.

"Davitch." the woman's voice whispered. "Davitch, you will be well. We will not leave you here to perish. We will love you. We will not let you die. You are so innocent. So sleep little boy; sleep. You are safe and we will love you."

The boy turned in his dream and all he saw when he opened his eyes in it was a warm gentle light. He was blinded by the beauty of it. It was inviting; soft and warm; like a heavy, luxurious, golden robe.

His dream deepened until the light began to fade.

He slept on until the light faded completely and he could feel the warm hands upon him. He knew in that moment that it was no dream.

Chapter One

"I am the cold floor. I am the slamming door. I am the child whore.
I will become a broken home. The shattered door. The open sore."

There is no greater hope than the hope of an orphan. Unless the greater hope is the hope of the dying. Whether it is a single orphaned child or a world of dying men; it is their hope that keeps them alive. But it is because they do not know what awaits them in this world or the next that makes their hope so painful, and so fragile; and makes their fear so desperate and so lonely.

But I was never alone. And neither are you.

We are all orphans in our own right. Some more than others, and others more than some; but we are all orphans. And in the quiet moments before we fall to sleep we often wonder if we are ever to find again that which we know in our deepest selves we believe we have lost forever.

We are all lost in our ways.

Only in my case now; it is more a metaphor than a truth; and in your case, it is more the truth now than a metaphor.

There has never been a time in the life of this planet when human beings have felt more alone, or more afraid, or more lonely, or more desperate. There has never been a time in your history when your hope has been so fragile, or caused you so much pain.

By the road I have traveled I would tell you of how I once came to be wrecked upon a beach, and near death, alone; yet in that place was surrounded by a warmth and a love I will in my poor way attempt to share with you now.

I can tell you as I begin that it was not my choice to live or die in a place such as that. I can tell you now that every orphan searches for it; or a place like it in his own way; yet few find it.

In the sad final moments before they flee their lives; they each look back and realize that little; if anything they did in their search for that place, meant much if anything at all. No one wishes on their deathbed to have spent less time living.

It is, ironically; in that moment, that we realize that in our own unique ways; we are in our own individual lives, each of us; all of us; wrecked upon a beach.

I can tell you that sooner or later, every single one of us will find our own way there. I can tell you how I met my life's journey's end in it. I can tell you also how I met an even stranger paradox; a beginning in that end.

This place I will take you to is real. It draws me gently back to it even as I begin this story to you. In fact, it is more real than the life you believe is real. It is more real than the fantasy you and all of us have created for ourselves. It is more true than the lie you have built around you and come to doubt at every meaningless twist and turn of your own fragile life.

For this is the Orphan Creed.

To go home again.

But really it is more. It is in its essence and has at its core a single purpose.

For the orphan whose life is fractured by his disbelief of everything that others would have him believe as true; it is a map.

For the orphan who grieves the home he lost or relinquished; or the orphan who laments the place that seems to have been taken from him; it is a coming home. It is the candle in the window. It is the warm bed, the sure embrace.

But there is a price to it.

There is only one way to regain that which was taken from you. Or thrown away by you.

It is simple.

In order to find your way back; you must bring at least one other orphan with you.

Leave no one behind. This is your charge. This is the price. If you take it, and accept it; it is yours.

You don't have to believe me. That really is the beauty of it.

But deep down inside, after you read this, you will believe me.

Every orphan who hears my story will believe me.

He will recognize the place I will take him to now.

He will know it and remember it; and in remembering it; he will find his own way home. This is the only promise I can make to him now.

He will find his own way home and I will wait for him there.

But all orphans are liars. Or so I've been told a hundred times. Orphans are criminals, liars and thieves and beggars and whores.

So given a choice; whom would you believe?

The son, or the orphaned son? Who is greater in the eyes of the Father?

Even though every rational part of you will argue with me, and the rational part of you that believes that you can't go home denies it; and screams at you from every fiber of your being that you can't ever go home; I tell you simply that you can, and that one day you will.

I know the way. I've been there. I'm here now as I begin this story.

I'm going back as it ends.

You need not believe me if you choose. You may believe me if you may. It was and always has been a gift to me. I keep that gift by making it to you now. Do with it what you will.

So you ask "Who am I to speak of this with such an irrefutable certainty?" "What great claim do I make to some mystical power or divine birthright to assure you that what I say is true?"

"None."

"I am more common than the swallow that nests in your barn."

"I am as inconspicuous as a leaf blowing in the fall."

"I have no pedigree."

"I have no education except the one given to me by life."

The only knowing I have is the one which was gifted to me in the place I will take you to.

My birth was as ordinary as a billion others before me and the billions of others to follow me.

The only distinguishing difference between those who are orphaned and those who believe they are not; if there is one at all; is simple.

It is the fact that those who are orphaned know they are orphaned.

If they do not know it, they are soon to be reminded of it.

If life does not teach them this; then the people in their lives will soon leap to the opportunities given them to teach those in their lives of their orphanhood.

Once you realize you are an orphan, you will realize that you did not create yourself. Once you realize you did not create yourself, you begin to ask the fundamental questions of "Who did?' and "Why?"

I did not create the circumstances of my life. They were created for me by something greater than myself.

More often than not; the circumstances of that creation can become ugly, stay ugly, and lead the way away from home.

Those are the lies I would have you disbelieve.

Some will ask of me my name or the place of my birth, or my father's name, or my mother's name. Some will wonder in the tiny consequences of my childhood play or the distress of my broken youth.

It is enough for me to say that I was born in the northern reach.

That's as specific as I need to be.

It's mostly a cold place where you wave to your neighbor but you don't really know much about him. Does that sound familiar?

It is a very human place that is insulated from the rest of the world for the most part by geography and language and religion. Most people here have never seen an ocean.

Most people here cannot make a place in their hearts for those who have.

It is a place that seems to have more than its share of small time politicians who believe they are big time politicians yet whose greatest crimes are stealing from their constituents by padding their part-time payrolls and exaggerating their mileage vouchers. Their greatest accomplishments seem to be measured in rusting park benches and broken promises. Does this sound familiar?

They can be easily recognized and can often be found drooling at the feet of senators and presidents; their lofty kings and queens; and their warped and fitful dreams are usually filled with lusty visions of power and wealth and entourage.

They are a sad lot mostly; reminiscent of mindless frogs in a shallow pond who pine always for a ruler to rule them; but yet who seem to eternally complain of the crane. Everything here is craftily sifted either though the webs of politics or economics. It is interesting to watch how little power it actually takes to corrupt them. Does this sound familiar?

Only no one wants to say so.

We have our share of gossips, too. Some of them work for the local newspaper. They are those poor in soul who seem to know so much of everything about everybody yet so little about themselves. They thrive on the misery and hardship of the misfortunate and the unlucky and the stupid. How empty would be their days without the obituaries of others?

We have our share of inept and scruple less lawyers who seem only to excel at cheating the little guys. They corrupt justice, not champion it. They do their best work behind the law, not in front of it. They are power hungry, greedy, treacherous people. Hungry for power; greedy for it, and mindless of the treachery it costs to obtain and keep it. They hate to lose, no matter what it costs them in soul.

What little integrity there is to be had in the meeting of their craft; they sacrifice in the selling of it. Their best efforts, it seems; are spent not in defending a law, or the accused; but in screwing their partner's wives behind their backs.

We have our share of crooked little businessmen who hide their vagaries at the little country club, or the little golf course, or the little banquet hall.

They occasionally get caught burning down their little restaurants; selling a little drugs under the counter of their little bar and grills; or they get caught with their little hands in someone else's little pocket.

In such a small place, it is difficult to hide. In such a small place it is difficult not to watch the drama of human existence unfold in such color and spectacle. Prophets and visionaries are not welcome here.

It's like a huge fish bowl where everybody gets to watch everybody.

It's a typical little blue collar town where ordinary people work hard because it's the right thing to do and their parents did the same thing, and their parents before them. But they never seem to get ahead because they are either too busy paying for their homes, their divorces, or their alimony, or their child support.

It's a place of seemingly long and endless winters that drive people to fever, madness, and stupidity; and often makes them all forget the promise of spring.

It is both a beautiful place and an ugly place. It depends on the eyes you use to see it through.

The summers here are warm and bucolic. But they were short for me it seems; and as a child; I looked for others like me. But there were none.

Orphans here are rare. Or they were silent. Or they had not yet awakened. I know that others like me are scattered across the face of this planet.

I don't know who they are or where they are now. I only know that deep down inside in that place where we all shiver at times; most of them are gone now. At least the ones I knew.

I know that some of them were found out and hunted down by life, and killed. Those totally helpless orphans. Fed to the evils of this world.

Innocence is not a treasure the human species values.

It is a commodity that is traded and sold, and in some cases rooted out and exterminated.

Some of them, perhaps many of them, have been taken by accident. Others have fallen or will fall to illness or disease.

Others simply could not or cannot bear the pain of this place and have ended their lives prematurely, or will take their own lives before their lives are even met.

My mother was one. She was an orphan. Her love was so deep that she could not see the beauty of this world through her pain in it. My brother was one. He could not bear the pain of this place as well. I could tell you about him, too.

But this is not his story.

I have survived. And so have you.

In my case; my birth parents were taken from me. My father was taken first; an ugly story at best, and then a few pain-filled years passed until the pain of his passing eased. Then there was just this empty place.

My mother tried to fill that empty place in her loneliness.

I didn't understand it then. I understand it now. Despair floods in like water past the sandbags we shore up against the flood. It doesn't work.

Life is filled with trapdoors and pitfalls and quicksands. My father's life and his anger and leaving was a millstone hung around the necks of those who loved him. Everything that came after that day was measured against it. Those are what I came to call the accidental departures. One never sees it coming.

First you get sucked in; then you get sucked down. Then you drown and its over. Its never pretty. The aftermath is even uglier. But you learn to go on.

Then time seems to pass and the memory of those events dulls and things seem to change. It is never really forgotten. They may not even necessarily get better. They just get different. So in a way it seems better. Sometimes different seems better but its not. It just gets different

Its just different.

My mother was taken second. She was what I learned to call an intentional departure. The pain becomes unbearable. You sink into the muck of that despair.

Like I said; just because things get different; it doesn't mean they get better. It drives you insane in what is already an insane world and you end up in what has already become an insane existence. And there is no saving yourself.

It is not as insane as it might sound. But it is cruel to those you leave behind; if only temporarily. She left me behind without ever saying goodbye.

The details of those losses are actually unimportant. They make for a fairly sad story in and of itself. But in the long and short of it, their lives, my mother and father's, gave meaning to mine. I loved them both.

So their short lives in context with mine had meaning as well. It is enough to say that they were loved and that they are missed. It was in their loss that I became an orphan in this world at the tender age of nine.

In human years, it is a dangerous age to be alone.

But I was never alone.

I can say in retrospect, that in the psychic trauma of that transition, I awoke one day to a harsh, unforgiving reality, forever transformed.

What little residue from the life I had known before I became an orphan was beaten out of me after I became one.

Some of you may understand what I mean.

If I were to pick something to compare it to; I would use a river whose course is changed by an earthquake. The earthquake moves a mountain from its foundation and blocks a river from its course. My life was like that. I wasn't the mountain. I was a river that flowed by it.

I was stopped briefly; backed up briefly; but only briefly.

Life does indeed go on.

It finds a way around, over, under, whatever. You can only hold it back for so long. And then it breaks out. Spreads out. Washes over. Overflows. Spills out. But it goes on.

Life did indeed go on. One learns to go on. There is no alternative. Go on or go away. Go on or get lost.

For me; becoming an orphan was a grand surprise. A great "What the Fuck!" in adult terms...but a "oh no.." in nine year old terms. It was the beginning of a new learning process; a learning process of welcoming, and a learning process of partings. It was a learning process of uprootings and transitions and changes.

I became a professional learner. I became a perpetual guest whose job it was to continually learn, absorb, and assimilate the customs of strangers in an ever changing and constantly unfamiliar world.

On top of that, I became a ward of the state and a source of income to be bartered and traded. This is where it became dangerous. Add the element of money.

The life of an orphan has a unique set of challenges that most children who become one are ultimately unprepared to deal with.

On the one hand; the younger the orphan; the better equipped he or she is (or unequipped because he or she doesn't have to deal with) his or her orphanhood. Not that they have more to learn; but that they have less to unlearn. Older orphans are less likely to be adopted for this reason. The mold has already been cast; so to speak.

"Do you have any boys that are....younger?"

On the other hand; the older the orphan; the more likely it is that he will remember why he was rejected. Better to be orphaned at birth than at nine. The odds of adoption climb astronomically higher the younger you are.

At some point, you become unwanted.

There is no hope of ever being adopted. It's not the same as foster care. Any orphan can tell you that. So the hope of adoption...It dies. It is the first of many hopes that die.

There is only the hope of a bed somewhere. A meal. Maybe a friend until you are old enough to fend for yourself.

I was on the fulcrum of childhood; teetering one way on the totter or the other when my mother departed. It could have gone either way.

For the ones who survive the initial shock; it becomes a test of will. It becomes a matter of will you or won't you? A matter of camouflage and adaptability. It becomes an evolving issue of observation.

In many respects, it reaches into the human condition at its most primal levels. For the orphan, the first level of awareness is a basic one; one of survival. If you don't survive, you won't make it to the next level.

None of the others will mean anything afterwards anyway if you don't learn to survive. Learn to survive. That means learn to observe. Learn to listen. Learn to keep your mouth shut. Learn to submit.

"Was I talking to you!!!!"

Accidents happen. You could fall and break something. You could walk into a door. You could bang your head. You could get in the way of something. Accidents happen all the time.

Everyone I met when I was a child seemed to know I was orphaned. They all seemed to adopt (no pun intended) a degree of suspicion and remotely; a posture of defense. I'm not sure why they did that. I never asked anyone to love me. It made me wonder why.

I know now. It was a question some of us ask all of our lives. It is a question most of us ask all of our lives. I don't ask it anymore. I don't need to.

Like most orphans, I met regularly with the extremity of both human kindness and human weakness.

I could describe at length both those kindnesses and the litany of abuses that stem from those weaknesses; but they are witnessed over and over again in brilliant and shining relief in our every day lives. I'll show you some of it; but not all of it. The rest of it you can wonder about or surmise on your own.

Human beings are so transparent at times. That's one of the reasons I don't need to point at them. You see them just as I do. I don't need to remind you.

We like to pretend that we don't see them. Who am I to steal that from you?

In fact, we really are good at pretending that we don't see them at all.

No one is ever really comfortable looking at themselves in a mirror; and those who are comfortable looking at themselves in a mirror are often considered mentally ill.

We do it often enough to appease our vanity; but we hardly ever do it to calculate our own moral inventory, or our own character defects, or our own personal shortcomings.

We like to hold the mirror up for others to look into; but rarely do we like to look into it ourselves.

Orphans are taught to look into the mirror. They are often punished with it. "Can you see yourself? Look at you!?"

They are often forced into and abused by Alice's Looking Glass.

Or we fall into a sort of personal looking glass that takes us to our own little wonderland.

Kind of like Alice in a way. Down a rabbit hole no one else can follow. "You must be mad, Alice. Everyone here is mad. You wouldn't be here if you weren't mad!"

But...and that's a huge but. Depending on the age of their awakening, orphans will see different things when they look into that silvered glass.

In my young understanding, in my early awakening, I saw all these attributes of strength and weakness; and many other things; reflected in my own human soul looking back when I looked into the mirror into my own lonely eyes.

I pondered how one could arrive at the edge of one's existence on a daily basis possessing in character any of these qualities. There has to be some value to them for us to cherish them as we do. Such was my thinking.

My greatest problem was not that I saw any of these things; because we all do at some point or another; but my problem was that I had no one to explore them with. I had no one left to teach me what they meant or what they were for.

In a way; that was both a good thing and a bad thing.

I got to choose.

I got to pick what I wanted to keep and what I wanted to throw away. Not everybody can say that.

It was safe to say then; that I had not as yet been molded into anything that even closely resembled a human adult. But I have been molded by someone.

The question you will ask yourself over and over again as you turn these pages will be but "By whom?"

When I first met her; I thought maybe I was dead. I thought somehow that she was my dead mother come back to life. I thought somehow that she had perhaps come to escort me across that barrier all men must one day cross; that I was dead and I had somehow made my way to paradise.

I thought I was an accidental departure.

The only thing that didn't fit was the excruciating pain I was in.

It didn't match the limited and sometimes comical description of heaven I had been led to believe was the promise for the innocent or the forgiven upon their passing from this life to the next.

Or maybe it was hell. That description was comical too.

Maybe the orphaned child inherits damnation. Maybe the unbaptized bastard child of dead fathers and mothers born into a loveless life dies and incarnates immediately into a lifeless hell.

Or maybe it's the other way around.

I was delusional when I first looked into the depth of her eyes. They were like a deep blue well that has no bottom.

I've also often wondered whether it was a dream or a nightmare.

I've also wondered whether her gifts to me have been a blessing or a curse.

This has been the nature of my life before I met her; and for the most part; it has been the nature of my life after I met her.

It has been both a journey of struggle to remember on the one hand; and a struggle in a journey to forget on the other.

But I would not change it even now. My life became undone even as it began. It is undone now... even as it ends.

I'm not really sure what it was that set me on the road that led me to that place. I was nine and I was alone. Bad luck? Good luck? Divine intervention? Divine comedy? Karma? Timing?

Who really knows? Does it really matter?

How many of us look back and wonder at the crossroads in our lives and wonder in the turns we could have taken? Where they might have led?

I remember standing speechless and tearless beside an open grave. I remember the handful of dirt that I held clenched in my angry fist as I watched a coffin that bore the dead body of my mother lowered into what became her grave.

I wondered in the depth of it. I was only nine. What else would a nine year old wonder in a moment such as that?

I wondered if my handful of dirt could fill it.

When I opened my eyes on that deserted beach; I thought I saw my mother's azure blue eyes looking gently into mine. I sensed that she could see I was injured. I could see she was injured. They seemed to say to me in the kindest of ways that I would go on.

But despite my delusion; I knew in my deepest self that my mother had died what seemed like a lifetime ago.

Five years after I dropped that fistful of dirt on her shining wooden casket; I wrapped a dirty old rope around my neck and tried to join her.

My failure in my unspoken pain and despair, and my unshared aching loneliness only served in adding to it. In looking back it becomes no great wonder to me at all that I began my life after failing to end it.

The greater irony, I suppose, is that my life was saved after almost being murdered in it.

This is just one of the great paradoxes of the road I have traveled. At almost every turn in my road there have been signs that have pointed in directions that have confused and confounded my every attempt to understand.

At every turn I see the hand of a greater power at work than I could ever hope to understand.

Perhaps now will I really understand.

It was winter when I ran. It was cold and bitter. I had just turned fifteen. I was a man. I was a young man. I had these horrible rope burns on my neck that took months to heal.

They became my painful, ugly reminders of the foolish struggle I had created between a desperate act of life and a certain act of death.

For me; just as they must be for other orphans who find that place of despair; they became a sensitive and visible accusation; a not-so-tender reminder of a place where I had the desire, but not the courage or the right to go.

The slow strangling choke of the rope I had, without success, tried to use to end my life was far worse than the constant desperate strangle of the unending loneliness that wrapped itself around my life in the first.

So instead, I ran.

Instead I offered myself up to a great unknown. I really had no idea where I was going when I left.

Away.

I was going away.

It was cold where I was and warm seemed the logical choice.

As if madness has any real logic to it.

The world and its madness was beginning to make a sense to me.

As if madness and its logic can have any sense to it as well. I was dying and in my heart, I knew it.

The mold had been cast. I did not fit. I would never fit.

The world is mad. It is insane and everything in my life was telling me so. How could I know? How could I see the horizon that awaited me? By that time I was blinded by my pain. I was numb. I didn't care. I really didn't care.

Nothing really mattered. So I ran away.

Between mirrors that show you that you do not fit and hand-me-down clothes meant to show you that you really don't fit; and abuse that proves that you are unfit; it was impossible to believe in anything else.

Most orphans, especially the older ones; learn early that they do not fit.

I was told soon after I ended my childhood and began my orphanhood that jail cells are "one size fits all."

It was a truth that was not lost on me, and one that echoed in my head on more than one occasion.

Running away was the first step that would bring me closer to one. I knew that escape was a threshold that would forever change my life once it was crossed. I also knew by then that the world was filled with predators who were as mad as the world which spawned them.

Someone once told me that orphans were actually adolescent predators who just hadn't had enough love beaten into them. Perhaps.

Perhaps.

In my young mind, I was running away because I did not fit. In my heart, I was running away because I was dying inside. In reality; I was running away because I had reached the end of my horizon in that place and there truly was no where left for me in my life to go; but away.

I suppose I wanted to get wherever life was going to take me. As harsh as it may sound; I wanted to get it over with as soon as possible. It just seemed like a less painful form of suicide.

Instead of killing myself; I'd let life kill me instead. It had already killed everything else I had come to love.

The pendulums of kindness and abuse were swinging wildly. There was no apogee or perigee of love in this world. If there was; I could deal with that. But it was like a comet of cruelty heading straight toward me. There was no getting out of its way.

I couldn't understand them. I tried. Maybe I should have tried a little harder. Who knows what road it would have led to had I been able to figure it out?

There was no discernable pattern or reason to them. There was no continuity to my life. My choices were hammered into me. When I didn't fit, the edges were scraped off, or pounded off, or burned off and I was made to fit. Orphans will fit somewhere, someday. Or trust me; one size will fit the one that either chooses not to fit; or for some reason, can't.

I ran because I didn't fit. I ran because my choice was to run or hang.

People are the same everywhere, mostly. When I got tired of running, I stopped. It was warm by then.

I hired onto the first ship that would take me.

Lying was one of the first things I learned how to do. Orphans are liars. So I lied about my age; but most people are liars and most of what people say are lies. They lie and they expect lies.

It is one of the great sadness' of this world that we have to teach our children the difference between the truth and a lie.

That particular sadness almost killed me. There are so many sadness' to overcome here.

The truth is not welcome in this world. The lie is promoted and paraded and exalted. It is rewarded, elected, and empowered. The liars rule in tyranny over the truth in this world.

Hanz was the first stranger that I met after I ran. I met a few others in passing; but Hanz was the first person I had the first real opportunity to observe in any great detail.

His warm exterior was a calculated deception meant to disguise a mean, aging closet Nazi who beat his Vietnamese wife relentlessly. I never knew her name.

When I first spoke with him he just smiled and smiled. He never said a word. He just smiled.

I never trusted him.

He never knew who I really was.

He never knew my name.

I had lied to him about that as well. All he ever knew about me was that I never trusted him.

He was the cook. He was a good cook; although I think his wife deserved more credit for the cooking than he did. She would cook and hide.

Sometimes I think he spit in my food before he handed it to me. Maybe that's why he smiled so much.

Some orphans learn that others will spit in their food before it is handed to them. They come to learn that they are not loved. The choice is to eat what is offered or go hungry. Especially if you know they've spit in it.

To refuse to eat what is offered is to insult the person who offers it. To insult that person is to invite that person's anger and wrath. To invite that person's anger and wrath is to accept the consequences that comes with it.

To know you are hated is to taste the spit in your food. Hatred; like another's spit; has its own unique flavor.

It is a spice much savored by our species and so common in our world that it would be sorely and immediately missed by many far more than its counterpart were it taken from our table.

As the cook, Hanz ran the ship's store with an exactness that reflected his German ancestry. He had this exacting, meticulous nature that was exceeded only by his propensity for brutality in all it's forms. There were times we could hear the rape of his wife through his cabin door.

She was this poor, tiny, broken creature who in my dreams took her vengeance upon him one sweltering night and fed him gagged and bound in one great feast up to the sea.

I watched that morning from the aft castle as he missed shot after shot. He had been shooting at them since breakfast. The dolphins were just out of range and seemed to be oblivious to the evil he was about. He was determined to kill one. Why? I have no idea. Just to kill something. It was who he was.

Hanz was tiring and couldn't heft the weight of the British Enfield against the rise and fall of the ships's bow with any degree of accuracy.

He was a weak man and like most weak people, he was just plain mean. I'd seen and been "fostered" by weak people before. They use belts or shoes to beat their prey. They use whatever tools are at hand to give them added advantage. When they tire, or when they finish with their sport, they blame their victims.

"You made me do it."

"You should have just kept your mouth shut."

The dolphins hadn't come for him anyway. They had come for me.

Besides Andre and the Chief Engineer, and Willy Eubanks; the dolphins were the only friends I had on the planet.

I hated Hanz.

It was ok to hate him then.

I don't hate him now. Of all the people I had met in my young life, he really was a soulless person.

In that moment, I wished he would just fall overboard and drown.

I don't know how many hours I had spent on the bow of the ship watching the dolphins play in the course of the waves.

We had been at sea for weeks. They had followed me. I was sure of it.

They were fluid and graceful, turning and rolling, each in their turn, smiling one after the other up at me.

I would smile back and wave and they would disappear in the foam only to reappear again fifty feet away. How many times did I wish to join them? Take me with you...please... take me with you. At night they would disappear completely to feed and sleep and do whatever dolphins do.

But during the day, they would come and play and make love and tangle themselves in front of me as if only to say that I had in some small way become their friend in another world.

I knew a little bit of their legends. I knew about the history of mariners and the relationship these gentle intelligent creatures of the sea had with seafarers. Many were the stories passed down of shipwrecks or sailors washed overboard who had been saved or taken to land by these graceful sentient beasts of the deep.

I cringed at every shot and smiled at every shouted epithet.

I knew it was the truth of his soul spilling from that filthy Nazi mouth. I knew when he swore, the vulgar ogre had missed again. "Keep swearing, you bastard," I whispered to myself. "Keep missing; I hope the gun blows up in your face."

But it didn't. The universe doesn't work that way. It has other designs in mind. It takes the most heinous acts imaginable; perpetrated by the ugliest creatures in existence; and turns them into something beautiful.

If nothing else, the universe is a study in balance; and when something is taken, something must be given. When something is found, something must be lost. It can be no other way.

Hanz finally found his mark.

I watched as the wounded dolphin leapt from the water and pin-tailed in a convulsing spiral into the clear blue of the warm waters of the southern reach. I watched the crimson red of its wound trace a bloody path like some ugly rope of scarlet stain into the depths. It was like someone had taken some obscene red ink and blotted it into a clear and cloudless sky.

I don't know how I got from the aft castle to the bow. All I remember is suddenly standing there smiling at Hanz. I was screaming inside. He thought I wanted to take a shot, maybe kill something; join the sport. I think in that moment I could have shot him. He thought I wanted to join in his cruelty.

Most cruel people think that their cruelty is acceptable. Some of them actually find their cruelty humorous. Bullies are like that. Until you beat their ass.

Ask an orphan how funny it can be.

That's one of the reasons why I ran away. The mold had been cast.

So I just smiled to Hanz and held out my hands.

He smiled as he gave me the rifle. I took it; admired it for a moment; and then calmly threw it as hard and as far as I could into the ocean in the direction of the dolphin he had just killed.

I'd seen the look a hundred times before. It is the incredulous face of disbelief. The look that immediately and viciously precedes the one of "Boy...you are about to get the biggest ass whipping you ever got."

I never had a problem calling the kettle black. Most orphans are good at that. They reach a point in their lives where they just know. Here it comes. "Boy, you done opened up a big old can of whip ass!"

They get tired of being slapped down. They get tired of being slapped, punched, kicked.

They know they are going to get it one way or the other so they might as well get something out of it.

So they just start calling it the way they see it.

My biggest problem was I didn't know when to stop calling the kettle black. I got to the point where I would call the kettle black and blue. I suppose I deserved some of it. I provoked some of it. I was a smart ass. Maybe. But I know I didn't deserve all of it.

"Son, you got yourself a bad attitude. And I'm going to adjust it for you."

"I ain't your son, Dad. Why don't you just adjust yourself?"

Maybe I should have thought twice on more than one occasion. Maybe I should have thought twice before heaving the rifle into the drink. Maybe.

He hit me so hard he knocked me down. Loosened a few teeth.

When I hit the steel of the deck; I was out cold like a cucumber. I don't remember when I hit the water.

I don't know what happened to Hanz, or Andre, or the Chief Engineer after that. I remember floating in the wash and seeing Hanz grinning, laughing, and waving to me from the stern of the ship as I struggled in the wake.

I remember thinking that he would probably beat his wife just a little bit harder that afternoon for my tossing his rifle into the ocean.

I remember thinking that I was going to miss lunch, spit and all, and it would probably be dinnertime before anyone noticed I was missing. I wasn't due on watch again until evening.

I remember thinking I would probably drown before nightfall and that no one would really ever know that I had been murdered.

The sea can be like that. Maybe that's why I sought it out. It had a size to it that scared me when I looked into it.

It reminded me of a hole I couldn't fill with a handful of dirt.

It had a depth to it that was beyond anyone's knowing and it appealed to me in a way I still don't understand.

Maybe it has something to do with horizons and what lies beyond them.

But I've always had a knack for being able to see just over the edge of them.

I was lucky I came to when I hit the water or I would have drowned outright. Or maybe it wasn't luck. Maybe it was just supposed to be.

I remember watching the ship disappear over the horizon and feeling the same sense of loneliness I had felt walking away from that empty grave five years earlier. I didn't think it was possible to feel a greater loneliness than I had felt that day.

But I was wrong.

I've been so wrong about so many things in my life that I'm still left with a world of questions.

"All in good time," she had said. "All in good time."

Chapter Two

We watched from a distance as the boy was struck and thrown into the ocean. It was not good. We watched the man who did this at other times throwing scraps of food from a pail off the stern of the ship. Our sight is keen, but our other senses are keener. We had never sensed or felt anything but benign indifference toward this man. But the boy was different. We had come to love this human child.

It was evident to us that he was in pain. We had noted this when we first made contact with his ship. He was on the bow. It was obvious to us he was in pain. We do not know the name of the ship he traveled on, and he has never said; or the year as you have come to count them; but we knew he was in pain. This much we could see. This much we could sense.

He was young as humans measure years; perhaps fourteen, fifteen. We were not certain. Human children grow so fast. But it did not matter to us. We could see the innocence of his heart, his soul; we could see it in the way he smiled, in his laughter, in his gestures to us.

We knew that he was good.

We wanted only to bring a joy to his heart; to make a fond memory for him. So we had come to play before him in the rolling waves folding relentlessly before his ship. We followed him.

Had we known what evil awaited Mara; we would have left the boy and the ship to sail on without our company.

We have interacted with humans in our past. We have helped mariners many times over the centuries that have come and gone since the Great Deluge.

Our race has saved many human men and women from a death upon the sea.

But this was the first human child I myself was given to help.

I would have made the choice even had he not endangered himself first by protecting us.

It has been our great joy to come and play in the crest of the waves rising before the ships of men. In this place where we live, we watch them as they come and go. We mark their passing in a peaceful, joyful exchange and wonder and leave them to their world as they leave us in ours.

We have shared many carefree moments in time with lonely men who labor upon the seas in the coming and going of their ships.

It is rare to encounter a human as cruel as the one who cast this boy into the sea.

It is certain he meant for the boy to die.

It is also certain that he meant for Mara to die.

Mara was my sister. Mara was the one who was killed by this man in his search for sport.

We do not decide who is to be helped when events cause a human to be swept away or set adrift upon the place we make our home. We were once human ourselves.

We let the Great Ocean decide who is to be found.

We let the Great Ocean decide who is to be lost.

When we find them, if we happen upon them; we do as our consciousness commands us to do. We honor life, no matter what form it takes.

But in the matter of this child, this boy, and the killing of my sister; it was indeed a grievous thing. It was a man from his ship that caused the death of my sister.

I would tell you of the moment in which it was decided among us that he should not suffer death for having come to our defense. It was decided in that same moment that he had earned a greater reward for the sacrifice which had put his life most certainly to risk; and without our help; most certainly to end.

There was no reason to suspect that the events of that day would unfold as they did.

Such do we sadly remember; and so are we so costly reminded; is the savagery of man.

Most of us settled into the deep when the life force fled from my sister.

Those of us who remained on the surface saw what happened next.

But it was not long after Mara's lifeless shell had settled upon the golden sands of the ocean floor that all of us heard the sound of the boy's body hitting the water.

This is his story and I will help him share it with you.

I am permitted, for I am Keeper of Our Way.

We are but a small part of his story. And I, as Mara's eldest sister, am given to share it with you.

We; those of us who remain; are each of us, but a small part of it.

So ours is his and his is ours. And what is ours becomes yours.

And I am weeping now as I begin. He will find his way home. This is what we charged him to do when we found him adrift; and in our time; set him back to shore.

We returned to the surface and circled the ship. We saw the man walk the length of the vessel; watching over the rail as the boy's unconscious body drifted past him. We watched as the boy regained consciousness and began his struggle in the white foamy wake of the propellers.

We watched as this man waved his cruel goodbye to this boy.

We will remember this man. One day we will forgive him. But he will remember his cruelty long after it has melted from our memories.

We turned in the foaming wash of the ship as it slowly plowed its way toward the southern horizon and searched in the wake for the boy. When we found him he was bleeding from his injuries and struggling to keep afloat.

He was screaming and waving for his ship to return. But he was alone. No one could hear him except maybe for the man who had set him adrift; us; and perhaps the predators who would soon taste and smell of his blood in the water.

The ship did not turn or slow from its course and soon the man on the rail disappeared into the rusting hull of the vessel.

So we turned our full attentions to the boy.

He was in a panic. Our presence only made it worse.

It became immediately clear to me that he would tire soon and drown and join my sister on the ocean floor.

I was so angry and saddened in that moment. All my thoughts were clouded by the blood of my dead sister. It had been such a senseless slaughter of such a beautiful creature.

The others, like me, were shocked and heartbroken over our loss. I could feel their anger toward this human child; toward humanity. I could feel it pulse through the water in rivulets of fury and pain.

I'm certain that the boy could feel it on some level as well. So they left the choice to me, withdrew silently; and moved away.

Looking back at that moment; it is unlikely that they would have chosen to help the boy.

Their anger toward him was misdirected; but it was a living thing in the face of the brutality that had ended Mara's life. I wouldn't have blamed them. But I would have carried the guilt of that inaction for the rest of my days.

It was my choice. They left it to me.

I am Eden. I am Keeper of our Way.

It was by my heart, and by my soul; that the decision was made that the boy should be spared a death upon the open sea.

There are many truths surrounding my decision in that moment.

It is true that I made this decision without knowing the identity of this boy. It is true that I did not know how it was that this whelp of a man had come to be upon a ship that plied its way upon our home.

There were many things I did not know in that moment before the decision was made.

I admit, that greatest of all; I did not understand how one of his people could leave him to die upon our sea.

Ebron and Sallon departed at my direction with Tesla and my youngest sister, Neva; to bring Mara's lifeless body home.

They were beside themselves with grief.

We; much like human beings; grieve our dead. We; loving as deeply as we love; feel our loss as much if not more; as you yourselves are drawn to do.

But we do not bury our dead.

Instead we offer them lovingly back to the sea which gives birth and then life, and then joy to them. The Great Ocean receives them back and returns some; but not all; to this place.

The manner in which this is done is known only to us; to the Great Ocean; and now to the boy.

It was I who first approached him. He had been in the water for the better part of the day. He had shed his clothing. Naked, he had been weakened by sun and thirst, and fear.

Even though our species shares a warmth of blood; his was slowly cooling in the warm waters of our home. I could feel his shivering as I approached. I could feel his panic rise to that of a mindless terror.

As I circled him; I looked into his eyes and recognized a life ending and I shared with him in that moment his human understanding of this. But it did not matter what I could see or feel and it did not register with him. The water was alive with his terror of me.

Perhaps in that moment he thought I had come to take some savage retribution upon him. Never in our long history has this been so. Though we have had much cause and many an opportunity; we have never harmed another human being.

Perhaps in that moment, a part of me wanted to.

But in all; I could see that he would not endure the night without my help.

The ship had long since disappeared and he was alone on a sea of glass. The setting sun was our only witness to the moment before us.

When I approached him, he made a last feeble attempt to evade me. What renewed life his fear gave him quickly faded in the darkness that fell like a curtain upon us.

I kept my distance until he calmed.

It became apparent to him; that had I intended to harm him; I could have easily inflicted it upon him.

His first touch confirmed in my heart that I had made a choice I would never regret. All I felt in his touch was his sorrow for my loss. As I felt this, he knew that somehow, someway; he would go on.

He took the grip I offered him, crooked his elbow across my dorsal, and he laid his naked body across mine.

In that moment we began a journey together that has lasted to this day.

We have many qualities that some human beings possess. We also have qualities that humans possessed at one time and have long since forgotten.

We are able to discern many things by the power of our touch. For us it is a wonderful thing; a joy that reminds us of the beauty of this world and the fading illusions of this life. We revel in the feel of each other because it reminds us of who we truly are.

In this one quality we are given to know the substance and the depth of another's heart simply by their touch. It is difficult. No. It is impossible to deceive us in this.

It is only one of many gifts we have been given in our lives within the seas.

So it was by the first touch of this child; this human man-child; that I knew his story would one day be told. I also knew that somehow the boy would live. I also knew that he would one day return to you and come to harvest many wonderful gifts in his life.

I knew well in that moment too; that my life would change because of him. I knew that the world would change because of him. I knew that both of our worlds would change because of him.

I was at peace with that beneath the stars and the weight of his body above me.

So did I come on a sad and grievous day to meet a human child that I have come to love as my own. By the sharing of his sorrow for my loss; he would in his innocence and love; seek to lessen mine.

He will help you to remember. He will teach you what the orphan knows. He will show you the way home. He will bring one of you with him. He will remember what we have promised never to forget.

It was I who brought the boy to the beach. I am Keeper of our Way and it was I who took upon myself the responsibility for the life of this human child. For the now he is yours.

But one day soon he will return to us.

He knows the way.

I remember that night well. The sky seemed to glisten with my grief.

The journey to my warren took many hours. The stars were fading from the darkened sky when I set him gently upon the sands of our lagoon. It is in this hidden place that we come to say goodbye to those that we love.

I gave him as much of my strength as I could spare in the darkness of those hours. He was near death by the time I laid him upon the beach; both by the salt of the water which he had consumed in his thirst; and by the warm waters which had sapped the remaining strength from his life.

What thoughts remained in him were delirious and dying.

The sun was rising anew as I turned and left him on the sand.

It was on that sunrise; and I shall never forget the wondrous beauty of it; that we said our fondest farewells to her who had been my sister.

I have often wondered what Mara would have thought of the silent witness to her farewell laying motionless in the sand in his deep and deadly slumber.

Many had come to say goodbye.

The ripple of grief that had spread from our pod had called others of our kind from the farthest reaches of the Great Sea.

Drawn by the throbbing ache of our loss they had come like racing, mournful messengers from deep and faraway places. The lagoon was alive with the voices of their grief and the whispers of their solace.

It hurts me to think now how common for us this ritual has become. All of them, each of them in their turn; passed by the human child; gazing in angry curiosity at the point of bleached sand where the boy lay half submerged; shivering and silent.

It seemed to me that each of them accused him of her death. But that was not the truth. His naked form could not have been more innocent of that crime.

I knew also that Our Way had been fulfilled by my bringing him to land. No one would have said more should he have been left to die where he lay. It was indeed enough that I had spent a night of my life in an attempt to spare his.

This has been Our Way for many centuries.

It has always been this way.

Mara's death confused us all.

When we find humans adrift in the sea; we try to return them to a shore; to the dry land from whence they come. We do not attempt to understand the reasons why they are set adrift or the circumstances under which we come upon them.

We only know that this has been Our Way since the Deluge.

We have always helped if we could; sometimes at peril to ourselves in battle with the great predators who wander these waters. But we have always helped if we could.

We are not always successful.

Some of those who find themselves adrift perish despite our best attempts to help. It seemed that with such a living anger toward this boy that this would be the case.

We do not decide and we cannot interfere beyond the shore. This has been Our Way since the Deluge.

We have made promises. We have struggled over the centuries to keep those promises. It has not been easy. Many have been the times we wished to break them.

But he was dying. I knew this. All who came to this hidden place knew this. Adding his death to Mara's was a torment to me that I sensed moved through the others.

Ebron was the first to acknowledge that the boy would die if left without help from his kind. By bringing him to this hidden place, I had unknowingly and cruelly guaranteed his death.

Ebron's genuine concern surprised me. But it was more than surprise. In his concern for the boy, I felt my loss for Mara wash over me like a mountainous rogue wave and I choked on the emotion that sprang in my heart.

Ebron was betrothed to my sister Mara. In all our individual pain of our loss; Ebron probably suffered and grieved the deepest. His observation spoke like a shining star to the depths of Ebron's love. To think that my sister was taken from it is a sweet pain I have carried with me from that day.

Sallon was bitterly silent and I could not blame him. He loved my sister too in a way that a grandfather loves a grandchild or children love each other throughout their lives as friends. Despite their great differences of age; Sallon and Mara had been immediate friends since Sallon had arrived from the Appa Sea.

They had been inseparable as friends. A single thoughtless, savage cruelty had ended a lifetime of loving friendship.

Neva, for her youth, was confused and silent. She had inherited from our father a gentle wisdom and a sense beyond her years, and she looked to me for an answer to this dilemma.

Tesla was inconsolable. She had been swimming beside Mara when the rifle shot had ended the life; the joy that was my sister. She was close enough to Mara to feel Mara's spirit flee in a desperate, agonizing apology and pain.

I myself was confused by the intensity and magnitude of emotion that was flooding into me from every corner of the lagoon.

I admit that I did not understand at first how the boy had come to be thrown into the water and left behind to perish a slow and certain death. I could not and still cannot fathom to this day the mindless cruelty which had ended the life of my sister and threatened the life of this boy in such a way.

I did not comprehend until I heard the boy stir upon the beach.

It is given to us to see and understand a great many things. In the whispered words of a shivering, dying human boy; I saw the sacrifice he had offered up to a savage man.

He had stood alone upon the bow of his ship; in the middle of a hostile sea; and defiantly rebuked a savage act.

For that foolish rebellion; and for the sake of creatures he could only love from a distance; he had been beaten and thrown to the sea.

It was indeed a savage man who had set him adrift.

I knew this to be a truth.

But in my heart, I knew the child had chosen in that moment his innocence instead.

To have stood by and said or done nothing would have made him as guilty of the act as the man who fired the shot.

For his poor fortune; for his defiance in our defense; his life would become forfeit as a result of it.

This was our knowing. This was our feeling and it spread among us like the ripples of our grief.

Even now in looking back it seems simple enough.

But the Great Ocean that gave birth to us all offered me no easy accord in the decision with which I was faced. But I am Eden. I am the Keeper of Our Way and I must keep it.

I did not owe this boy anything. I brought him back to land. I fulfilled that which has been our nature for thousands of years. I was almost certain that I had done enough.

I was almost certain.

But the truth is never as simple as it is certain.

He would die and he would die alone. That much was certain. That much was true.

He was to pay for the saving of one of our lives with the loss of his own. This was his fate. This was his destiny.

I could not accept his fate any more easily than I could accept my sister's untimely end.

There was nothing I could do to change Mara's destiny.

In my grief I would gladly have exchanged one life for another. I would gladly have chosen Mara's life over this human life and never have given thought again about him. Had I a choice, I would have left him to drown.

Had it meant a chance at saving my sister from the death she met at the hands of a man who was beyond the reach of my grief; I would have taken it.

Had the man who fired the shot fallen into the water accidentally, I would have kept him alive for days; only to feed him finally piece by piece to the sea.

I would have taken pleasure in watching him die of thirst.

I would have broken every vow I have ever held and lived my life by to taste that sweet revenge.

I would have given anything to have saved my sister from her fate.

These were the things I thought of as I wept.

We have many gifts. To feel. To love. To grieve are but a few of them. These gifts make us much as you are. But we know the well from which they spring. We know the time from whence they came. It is a time that is clouded in the minds of human memory. But it is fresh in ours because we keep it so.

We have preserved many things through the slip of time so that one day we might draw them from the Great Ocean and have them known once again by humankind. This mindless act made me question our service to this purpose.

So I did what my anger and my grief demanded that I do.

In the cold and heartless shadow of Mara's pointless execution and in the shining warmth and light of that child's selfless act; I decided that the boy would live.

I decided that he would be rewarded with gifts that would make your human understanding meet with ours. And in the meeting of our understandings, he would find his way home.

So it was by nightfall on that second day, that I came to make another decision. One that had not been made in centuries. One that had been forbidden us in the promises we keep.

There is a price to pay for the breaking of a promise.

There is a price to pay for crossing the bridge from sea once again to land. So it was in the falling, setting of that sun that Eden came to kneel beside the orphaned boy upon that beach.

This is his story and I have come once again into his mind to help him share it with you.

For I am orphaned now as well.

Chapter Three

"I am leftovers served. I am the unloved misfit in your hair."
"I will become a lonely, loveless criminal within your care."

I have known great rejection and judgement in my life. I know what it is to be both defenseless and to be judged. Many have been those who have leapt to fierce defense of what fragile humanity remains alive in me. Many have been the times as well, that I have been left to defend myself.

To be enthusiastically clubbed into a dreamless dominion is to know what it is to be truly defenseless.

Knowing well the grand irony of my life and the magical, almost mythical turns it has taken; I smile now as I hear her voice once again. I laugh to myself as I observe that perhaps my worst nightmare is about to manifest itself. The unwanted, orphaned child is again about to appear on my doorstep.

How many years have come and gone since she and I have spoken?

I will leave that for you to decide.

"Is your education in the world of men complete?" she asks.

No. I mean. I am self-educated; yes. I suppose. They have nothing left to teach me. Yes. I am finished here.

Yes. I suppose. If you will charitably count the stolen, occasional respite I found in warm, clean, public libraries scattered across the face of the earth as transcript of attendance in one of life's greatest and purest pleasures.

The next time you find yourself in a public library on a bitter cold day, or in the middle of a raging thunderstorm, or blizzard; look to see if you can find me, or others like me huddling there, trying to blend in among the armchair philosophers and learned scholars seeking to know just a bit more.

Mans' consummate desire to know, and his pack-rattish need to store and preserve his knowledge in libraries for posterity is divine in origin, and measured only by the people found searching for knowledge or a higher purpose or service within them.

There were many nights of tremendous fortune that I found myself accidentally locked inside them. "Oh Damn! I'm locked inside this nice warm library! What shall I do? Oh my!"

I wanted to learn. I was forced, like so many others, from the place of my birth. My home was torn from my hands. The friends I had loved in school were aches in my heart. But I loved school and learning. I learned early on the run that libraries, much like schools, are relatively safe places.

The few times I was caught inside after they closed were of such minor consequence that I was generously forgiven in a simple if not altogether truthful explanation. The most punishment I ever received was a gentle scolding. Perhaps the many gentle nights of unmolested slumber that I spent in them, coupled with the leaching process of osmosis resulted in my education?

Librarians are Keepers of the Light. Much like Eden was Keeper of the Way. It was free. I was broke. It was safe and warm. There were far more upsides than down sides to it.

I managed to read in a voracious, frantic, surreptitious search to understand my life, and all that had happened to me; many of the great works that others facetiously only claim to have read when they want to sound smart at a party or the ones they pretend to have read when they are making a toast, or running for office.

Stuff like Plato, On the Soul's Immortality; Socrates, Pythagoras, the epic poet Homer, his Iliad; not the artistic Winslow, 1836-1910; although I do appreciate his particular form of expression. Plutarch; The Bhagavad Gita, the Vedas, the Sutra, the Talmud. The Bible, the Koran, and many, many thousands of others that were all drawn gently into the sponge of my heart over the years in my simple and unending and all consuming quest to find some meaning or some answer to my trials.

They were mostly "to be or not to be" issues in the beginning. Then

I stumbled onto Milton who himself had lost his own paradise and had quipped that he would rather rule in hell than serve in heaven. Dante's Inferno. His Rings of Hell. My rings of hell. My inferno. I wondered at times if I wasn't some cosmic joke and already walking in some ludicrous, insane hell designed specifically for me. If it wasn't; someone sure went to a lot of trouble to make it look real.

Freud. Sometimes a cigar is just a cigar and an orphan is just an orphan.

In those early years after I returned to the beach, I focused mostly on the philosophical; the religions. I never traveled far without some form of literature tucked in my pocket or my backpack, or wrapped protected in a coat or a shirt.

People I met in my travels would walk up to me and hand me books and say "I'm done with this, read it." and walk away.

I'd be reading over a greasy meal in a greasy diner, or on a bus somewhere to nowhere and a book would magically appear, abandoned much as I was; and say to me in its own way, "take me, read me, take something from me."

I am, and always was, reading.

Cereal boxes, bubble gum wrappers, stuff like that, dictionaries.

I have lived in some libraries that would make the greatest minds on earth pause like frightened does in the headlamps of an oncoming freight train. Not because they were so big.

But because the sum total of knowledge represented in the tomes found in these libraries represented things they would never, ever be able to know; no matter how long they lived.

Their human lives are just too short. By the time they get to a point where they go "AH HAH!" They die! Kind of a cosmic joke on them, really.

I taught myself to speak an eloquent and hauntingly beautiful language with a book intended to do just that. It was loaned to me by another generous compassionate orphan; who herself was lost; and found it to be one of the most useful tools I have ever learned to use in this life.

I speak several dialects of that language fluently today.

I believe I would rather be blind than illiterate. And now I am.... But I am going home. Where vision is more important than sight.

But I had many teachers.

Some of them were young and some of them were foolish. Others were old and wise. But in many ways reading was my great escape from the brutality of my young life.

Orphanhood is like a broken glass. You can still drink from it. It is a life of sharp corners and even sharper edges. For some it is a life filled with cuts and bruises, broken bones, and even accidental or intentional departures.

Reading helped take the edges off some of those corners. In some cases, the book itself became my teacher.

Someone once remarked to me that what each orphan needs to survive is a single person to love them come hell or high water. I know that hell is a metaphor. It can come while you are alive. It can come when you are happy or sad. It can come and the water can rise.

I know too that one person can love an orphan into surviving.

If I am nothing more than this; I am proof of that.

That person also remarked that; in the grand scheme of things; especially on this planet; children are the point of it all. I'm not sure what that person meant by that.

I have always felt that we are all children regardless of our age, each of us.

So I questioned it for a very long time. Are they? Are children the point of it all? Are they indeed?

I suspect that there are a few exceptions to that rule. There are always exceptions. What do we live for, if not for our children?

So I'm going to take one. I will take exception to the rule and open just a tiny crack in the broken window I see my life through.

All you really need to know at this point is that I was a child once, and perhaps, maybe just perhaps, in many ways; I still am.

Granted. I am an orphaned child; if that matters. It might. I don't think it should.

I want you to know, though, that I didn't become who I am overnight. No one does. I became who I am through a painstaking ordeal of trial and error.

In this will I take the boldest of liberties with you.

Having opened that broken window; climbed out of it; and set off every kind of alarm there is to set off; I will let you walk; no...we better run... in my steps for but a brief moment to see just how far you can see, see, see; in the depths of my deep blue sea, sea, sea; and I will beg beforehand your mercy if I have in taking this risk made an unforgivable mistake.

Shall we? Don't worry. I will bring you back. Let us run...

One day in a pitiable, self-indulgent exercise in anger, I purchased a handsome, three piece crushed denim Levi suit. When I bought the suit, I also purchased a beautiful embroidered ivory Arrow shirt with abalone buttons, a crafted narrow cream silk neck tie, and the only pair of genuine calfskin penny loafers I have ever owned.

I had the suit custom tailored and the luxury of the crushed blue denim made me feel warm and successful. It came with a vest sewn with heavy brass buttons that, when I touched them, felt strong and confident and certain.

The shirt had delicate golden filigree stitching that reminded me of a time in a place and a robe that I had once worn in what seemed to me to be a lifetime ago. The buttons of the shirt were carved of abalone shell and reminded me of the shining opulence of pearls. The tie was a rope I had once wrapped around my neck.

The shoes were just shoes, but they were new and I filled the penny slots with shining new pennies as if to say that nothing better would do.

To know the truth is to know that I had shamefully begged, borrowed, and stolen the money for the clothing in a careening, uncontrollable, unexplainable desire and compulsion to return much like a dog to his vomit, a place I knew deep in my heart I had no right or business returning to.

When all was complete, I wrapped the costume I had constructed; the richly fragrant suit, tie, and shoes in plastic and rolled them carefully into a vintage woolen bedroll that I had bought in an army surplus store.

I wore the only change of clothes I owned and set off on a 1500 mile journey around a corner of my life. I headed with singleness of purpose toward a ritual I knew would soon take place.

It took the better part of a week on the road to make that journey. When I arrived at my destination, I found that many things had changed in my absence. Buildings had been torn down and new ones built in their place. New stores had opened and others; older ones, had closed.

But a river that I had once fished as a boy still flowed through this place and still held its secret retreats for me; and it was there in one of those secret places that I made my camp while I waited for the coming days to unfold.

On the morning of the observance, I bathed in the murky waters of the river that had always been my friend and shaved the post-pubescent stubble from my face as best I could. I dressed in the finery that I had purchased, and walked stiffly and self-consciously toward another awakening that I had no clue awaited me.

I found and took my place among the stands of the observance. I watched as proud parents and siblings and assorted relatives and friends assembled. I recognized teachers from my childhood who came to watch and participate in this venerable rite of passage. I was a spectator and no one really paid any attention to me at all.

I was a leaf among a pile of leaves.

I had chosen a seat that would permit me to search the faces of the graduates as they filed past me. I was close enough to smile to each of them and nod approvingly if I chose. I should have looked in a mirror first, because, oddly; being of the same age as the graduates; I didn't quite seem to fit into the picture of the parents and participants sitting proudly in the stands.

I even went so far as to address some of them by name as they rustled by me in their caps and gowns on that very special day.

Those whose eyes I managed to meet and briefly capture glimmered with a fleeting, confused, and contradictory recognition. A few, a very special cherished few; stumbled in startled surprise. When they turned back in seeing me there, they sent a visible ripple up and down the file of graduating students.

I watched in mixed and churning emotion as they made their way to their seats upon the graduation platform and nudged each other, nodding; whispering; and pointing my way. Their awareness of my presence sent a palpable tremor up and down the neatly arranged aisles as I smiled nervously toward them.

I had been absent from my desk in school for 32 endless, starving, lonely months.

I don't know and can't remember the exact moment when I wished I hadn't come. But I did reach it.

As the speakers began to speak and the singers began to sing and as the Salutorian and Valedictorian droned on hypnotically about the warm and poignant road behind and the bright and promising road ahead; I rose like a puppet and stood.

As I stood, so too did a putrid gorge begin to rise in my throat. I felt feverish with the stifling, cloistering, humid heat and then felt claustrophobically trapped in an outfit that suddenly felt clownishly out of place. I became nauseated to my bowels and suddenly and breathlessly aware of my own self-betrayal.

I turned and began to make my way slowly to the doors.

I could feel their every eye upon me. I could hear a thousand unanswerable questions waiting; clamoring in my mind like a clutch of looming vultures if I stayed.

What was it I felt emanating from them in that moment? Was it curiosity? Was it pity? Was it a curious pity? Or was it a dimly remembered affection?

To this day I wonder. To this day I still do not know.

When I reached the doors; I looked over my shoulder to the friends I once had loved a thousand counted days in my past. A thousand days. A prison sentence. I paused just barely long enough for all of them to see my tears. I didn't care that they could see them. Then I turned my back on them and in a sweating, feral fury; shoved the doors violently open and broke wildly into the bright June sunshine of a day that was never meant to be for me, or ever meant for me to share.

I ripped the tie off first, like the rope in a strangle, and threw it to the ground as I left.

I half walked, half ran to the river where I had made my camp in a bleary fog of tears. When I got there and saw the sum total of my existence represented in the few possessions waiting for me; I stripped as if my clothes were suddenly on fire.

Such was the force of my self-loathing and fury that the brass buttons of the vest audibly popped into the weeds; the threads breaking and firing like some second rate honor guard at my own solitary funeral. The buttons of the shirt in their turn sounded ominously like distant gunfire as the beautiful abalone shell leapt in crazy, harmless trajectory from my heaving chest.

And then I stood, naked in the sun; driven quite mad by my aloneness; weeping and laughing uncontrollably.

I looked upward through my tears to the bright blue cloudless sky and drew double fisted from my naked breast the most eloquently profane benediction I could stir from the cauldron of acid I called my heart.

I cursed God, each and all of them. I cursed the Romans, the Greeks, the Christians, the Muslims, the Jews; I cursed them all for letting me believe any of it mattered one small bit. I cursed Eden and her brood. And then as a fitting baptism into my anger and my shame; I urinated lewdly on the beautiful crushed denim suit and ivory arrow shirt, swaying my hips and playing the stream of urine while I hummed a wounded, caricatured, grieving pomp and circumstance.

I squatted, did a finale on the cheeks of my ass, and grabbed the penny loafers complete with shining new pennies, and clapped them like cymbals.

Then I hauled back and heaved them as far as I could into the silent, accepting, passionless, gaping maw of the river that had been my friend.

I dropped to my knees and wept. I was alone. I was nine again. I was alone again. But I was not alone. I was never alone.

I dressed in the sweat soaked filth of my road worn rags, washed the tears from my face in the warm silty effluence of the river that had always been my friend, and left the suit that was not me and never would be me in a saturated, stinking heap and headed away.

I walked that day. Hungry and hurt. I wanted to walk. It took the pain away. I wouldn't have to make small talk with strangers if I walked. No questions, no lies. I was incinerating in my self-inflicted humiliation anyway.

I walked and wandered that day. Burning in the dry dust of a road that was again at least another 1500 miles. I had spent an hour of my life shining like some incandescent, toothy fool; an uneducated sophomoric scarecrow out of some savage Land of Oz who was too stupid or stoned to know he didn't belong or didn't fit. For every moment of that mockery, I owed the universe another thousand miles. For each brief and fleeting second of that self-betrayal, I owed the road a thousand steps. It was a long day and I don't remember how it ended. I only know that it did.

I walked that day and blazed bold new trails into my hurt; each step pounding my pain to exquisite completion and peening into the radiant luminescence of my loneliness a servitude of a new order of magnitude.

I had graduated onto a new plateau of bitterness that I would be many days; even years; exploring.

Though I had swam in the river; I knew then, I believed then; that there was no going home. Eden was a dream. She was a long forgotten nightmare.

My life was an unending nightmare. My life, just like the river; was sweeping me before it. And just like the river, I had no thought and didn't much care as to where the current carried me or to where I would be swept.

It seemed to me then that the age of my youth had passed; though I realize now that it had passed long before this.

In my confused and shallow understanding and realization did I see my life as changed irrevocably. In this did I embrace my bitter fate as final and absolute.

The compelling resolve with which I had made my journey north had withered in the heat and I had no course by which to steer. In my haste to leave, I had chosen the barest of direction; south. A point on a compass. Away. Simply, mindlessly, away.

How many times in my life have I flipped a coin at a crossroads and taken the toss as my direction? I couldn't tell you.

Many. Legion.

I did not believe on that day that I would ever return here. In the virulent sarcasm of my inner monologue of that day; I recited a noble litany of colleges I would; given adequate incentive; bestow my learned presence upon. Yale, Harvard, Berkeley, MIT; even better yet, Oxford, as a Cecil Rhodes scholar no less.

My bitterness ate slowly away at me.

I could not stop the hemorrhaging.

The world; my human world; had inflicted yet another blow.

In all reality; I had in my own vanity and stupidity done it to myself. No matter what anyone says, this world is out to kill you. We are out to kill ourselves. Everything we do points to it. Or at least it did for me.

Everything I touched turned to dust. I wanted to go back but it wasn't time yet.

Everything I had learned up till then had warned me against it.

Why I did it I will never know. How I survived it is an even better question.

It was in Kentucky I think; or maybe Virginia; I'm not really sure; that I met again the face of kindness on my road.

I had been waiting out a pelting rainstorm on the interstate. I was the guy you passed standing with his thumb out under that overpass. The one with the bedroll. The one looking like life had worked him over pretty good. The young guy that looked ten years older than he should have been. That was me.

A sympathetic truck driver had given me a ride somewhere in Indiana maybe.

I rode several hundred miles with him as he talked incessantly about his home, his kids, his wife, his girlfriends, the dangers of hitch-hiking. I nodded in and out as he spoke. I couldn't help myself. The soft hum of the wheels and the twanging, guitar like intonation of his voice was a soft and rocking lullaby in my exhaustion. I'd been on the road for days.

Occasionally I would utter an "uh huh" or a "that's nice" and drift off back to sleep. He was kind and he knew I was exhausted, so he let me sleep.

There have been others who would have tried to molest me or rob me, but he just let me sleep. I knew it was rude, but exhaustion overtook me.

When he stopped at the exit, I stumbled awake. As he let me out he handed me a bag with thirty or so pills in it and said, "Stay awake, kid. It's a dangerous road yer walkin!"

It started raining shortly after he let me off. I waited for two endless, eternal days underneath that overpass; hitching, but cursed somehow. I was becalmed. Like some ship of old that hits a spot on the ocean where the wind does not blow and everything falls still.

For two whole days there was no ride, no wind to be had; no food, no water, no place to sleep, no toilet, no one to talk to. I was becalmed.

I had the rain as my companion and the steady stream of passing cars to remind me of how unwelcome I was in all their worlds.

The amphetamines the trucker gave me kept me awake, and kept my hunger at bay; but they made me sick with thirst. I would walk to the overflowing, gushing runnels from the overpass above and cup my hands and drink the oil tainted, metallic tasting runoff.

The pills called to me. They whispered to me of a release that a part of me could only dream of. It couldn't be anywhere near as bad as the rope had been. That's what I thought. But I would never intentionally end my life in such a place.

I had a gnawing fear of such a death.

I had seen before what the ravens and crows had done to the murdered bodies abandoned in the alcoves of overpasses such as these. I no longer climbed the concrete slopes looking for an unmolested place to rest. I would rather stand all night long on the side of the road than look and find something I would wish I had never found.

And the motorists. The warm, comfortable motorists driving by. How many of them had a sandwich in their hands? How many of them had a thermos of coffee? How many of them looked at me and feared an ambush in the solitary figure abandoned on the side of the interstate?

Some didn't even see me. I was an apparition; a figment of my imagination, not theirs. Some looked beyond me, through me, and drove on in quiet, silent indifference past the ragged illusion on the side of the road.

For others, I was a momentary entertainment. A distraction that stood out like a pothole or a speed bump on an otherwise unremarkable stretch of road. They would look intently and then look away pretending that they hadn't noticed me. Others would swerve to make me hop or jump, and I could hear them say in their cars, "Ha! Made ya jump!" I could feel the malevolence at times.

Occasionally a beer or soda bottle would come whickering magnetically toward me, sailing softly past my head to smash explosively against the concrete slope of the overpass abutment.

"HEY! YA MISSED ME!! Ya MISSED me. Come on back. You miserable, spineless, puke. You missed me."

But they would be gone forever. The universe my only witness to the viciousness of that random act of mindless violence.

When the rainstorm broke on the morning of the third day, I moved off down the road. I walked for several miles until I came to a truck stop on the opposite side of the interstate. I dodged the cars on the eight lanes of traffic and made my way across the burnt grass to the eastern edge of the freeway.

The restaurant was predictable. It was filled with aging, potbellied truckers wearing 200 gallon cowboy hats trimmed in dyed ostrich feathers and ludicrous, obscenely suggestive, oversized belt buckles the size of Texas. There were tired fathers towing tired mothers towing tired cranky children. There were tourists in every pastel color of pantsuit that K-Mart can sell.

And there was me.

I had been awake for days; standing, breathing car exhaust and drinking poisoned water. The amphetamines had pushed my ordinary caution of places such as these to an edge of unreasonable paranoia. I needed to put something in my belly or I knew I would collapse soon. I hadn't eaten in days. I needed to sit, to rest, if only for a moment.

No one even paused to look up at me as I made my way to the cafeteria line. It was almost as if I were invisible. Hey, everybody, a ghost just walked in. No. A skeleton that looks like a ghost. No. A human being that looks like a skeleton that looks like a ghost just walked in.

Nope. Seen one of those and he aint it. Back to my breakfast.

"Honey, can you pass me the ketchup?" "Yes, dear."

"Joey, stop hitting your sister!"

"Hey Bob, what ya hauling to Kansas?"

"I'm hauling ass, Bill. How about you?"

I had three dollars left to my name.

Not to infer, of course, that my name was worth three dollars.

Three measly dollars.

Truck stops are like airports. There is very little you can buy in a truck stop with only three tiny, crumpled, sweat soaked, itsy-bitsy, teeny-weeny dollars. And if you don't buy anything, well; that's loitering.

Loitering is against the law.

Unless of course you are loitering in a library.

There was also the small problem of body odor. I could smell myself. I had been on the road for days. My clothes were stiff with dried perspiration. I wondered how long it would take before I was talking with a State Trooper from this particular state.

I thought about the rest of the pills in my pocket. I had a dozen or so left. They would definitely be enough to get me a room for a night at the crowbar hotel; or two, maybe a month; maybe more.

But I was already in line.

The cashier had already sized me up.

She was watching me like a hawk.

She had watched me finger the bills.

It wasn't like I was fingering her.

I looked at her. She looked at me.

"Whatcha lookin at babe?" I thought to her as I looked at the cooling greasy, picnic fare.

Oh. I get it now. Can you smell me yet? Not close enough, huh.

She snapped her gum impatiently as I stood in the chrome railed protectorate of her domain. She never once took her eyes off me. I looked behind me.

I thought maybe I was holding up the line.

Nope.

Nobody here but us sweaty, stinking, runs like a chicken.

Of everything laid out on that cafeteria line, the only thing I could taste was her suspicion.

She looked at me as though there was something there that was really worth stealing.

I admit I looked the part.

I reached for a half-pint of milk and grabbed a powdered jelly donut. I met her eyes as I handed her the bills and smiled a lurid, murmuring hello to her breasts. "Keep the change darling."

I figured if that didn't get the State Boys rolling; I'd be alright and be able to rest in peace for as long as I could make the milk and donut last.

Her face never changed, but I could see her eyes smoking in naked embarrassment.

"Thank you." She said, snapping her gum to punctuate the rolling, descending tinkle of the change as she threw it into a bowl marked "Tips" beside the register.

I have a tip for you, sweetheart. Lay off the lipstick. If you smile, you're gonna get some on both your ears.

I swear she couldn't have been any colder. The milk in my hand seemed to drop in temperature by five degrees.

But she had kept my change and I had bought her for it. I had bought her silence for a handful of change. It was worth it.

Now I was broke. But I was free. At least for the moment. The minute I walked away from the cafeteria line I felt a pang of regret. But it wasn't really regret I felt. I felt something. Right between the fifth and sixth vertebra. Like a bayonet.

She started it.

I finished it.

She couldn't know that I had heard her thoughts.

She was judging me.

There. How do you like it, bitch? How does it feel to be owned? She knew it. For a handful of change no less. Like so much meat.

How does it feel? Do you like it?

Then stop doing it.

I didn't do it very often. I never liked how it made me feel afterwards. There was too much power in it, and I hadn't learned how to use it with any wisdom at all.

I was walking away from her and I could feel her hating me.

It pushed into me like a cold blade. I supposed I deserved it.

She was sharing the hate she felt for her life and the humiliating service she had to mete out in tiny measured increments of defiant politeness to unwashed, uncouth, leering strangers like me.

"Here, have a little some of this with your donut."

But in that cold blade she shoved into my back as I walked away; she really, truly, hated me. For what? Why? What did I really do to you? I had earned her hatred for a palm full of change?

It was a poor exchange.

She wasn't going to call anybody.

She was going to get off her shift and make an extra hundred bucks giving a few blow jobs to a few truckers in the VIP lounge before she went home to her husband and kids.

Somehow she knew I knew. That's really why she hated me.

I made my way to an empty booth beside a window that looked out on the freeway. It was almost noon and the place was crowding. I wouldn't be noticed. That's what I thought. I figured I had an hour, maybe two before the place began to clear.

I learned early the danger of men's eyes. I had perfected a humble, ground gazing countenance that allowed me to observe my surroundings in a periphery. It also occasionally helped me find things that other people had dropped accidentally but mostly it kept me from having to meet the eyes and minds of other men.

In the world of strangers, in the world of men; very much like in the wild; to meet another creature's eyes was to challenge it.

A stare, however brief, was an act of dominating, unforgivable, foolhardy aggression. Unless of course you happened to be bigger, or meaner, or faster, than the creature you happened to be staring at. Its either looking at eating you or you're looking at eating it.

I had been enthusiastically thumped more than once for that honest, inquisitive mistake. "You got a problem with those eyes, chump?" Here we go again. You get the picture?

Females are different. Their eyes tell an entirely different story. There are, of course, a few exceptions.

The window would give me pause to consider my situation in dry warmth and relative comfort. I needed to bathe. I reeked of sweat and exhaust and I needed to sleep badly. The amphetamines were an artificial, dangerous alternative to rest that induced a paranoia I never liked or understood; but one I was willing to endure to make my way back to a place I was familiar with as quickly as I could.

I turned my gaze from the window and the brightness of the glare and looked at the ridiculous sparseness of the meal before me. The powdered jelly donut was days old, but I had eaten worse. The milk would calm the mild and unrelenting nausea the oil tainted water had blessed me with days before.

I was in fine shape. Couldn't be better.

I closed my eyes and held my throbbing, aching head in my hands; and was genuinely glad to be finally free of the carbon monoxide of the road. I chuckled at my predicament and the appearance of comedy in the resemblance of a motion of a man about to say a grace over a stale donut; and so I said one.

One I had learned as a child. A simple grace I had learned in kindergarten by rote. "God is Great. God is Good. Let us thank Him for this food."

I didn't mean it. I was being sarcastic. I had closed my eyes because they hurt. I was holding my head because it hurt.

My whole life hurt.

I hurt. Everything hurt. I was dazed and confused. I was going to wolf down the donut; wash it down with the milk; and hope I didn't throw it up all over myself before it had a chance to begin digesting. It was no more sinister than that.

A distant voice drew me out of my daze. A grizzled, strangely gentle voice speaking directly to me. I was hoping I was mistaken.

Cops. She called the cops. The bitch called the cops. I'm busted.

Then a hand on my shoulder. Yup. The Boys in blue.

I'm busted. Been here. Done this. But the hand was soft in its weight, almost electrical in its touch. I turned; saying nothing; my head still resting in my hands; and looked sideways up into an abyss.

An old man stood next to me casually with his outstretched hand resting lightly on my shoulder.

I have to say that touching a stranger took some salt on his part.

Someone else might have taken his hand; broken it off at the wrist; and handed it back to him.

A woman of similar gray stood smiling next to him.

I tried to find him and know him in the glowing coal black of his eyes.

He just smiled as if he knew that he would not be found. I waited for him to break the stare; but it was I who finally yielded. This was no cop. This was something else. What now? Come on.

It was out of respect for his age I suppose, more than anything. I looked back at my donut and milk. Ok. What now? The guy was gray. He was going to tell me something. He had my attention. He knew that. I was going to listen. He knew that, too. He had me cornered. I hate spectacles. I was hoping this man wouldn't make one.

I didn't take it. I can't fix it. I don't know anything about it. And no, I don't know your kid; I'm not your long lost nephew; and no, I'm not interested in a threesome with you and your wife.

I picked up the milk carton and started fidgeting nervously as he began to speak. Go ahead old man, you've got the floor. Make the best of it and have a nice day. No; I don't need a ride. I'm actually heading the other way. I dodged 85 cars to cross the highway and get here; but thanks for asking. I'm smarter than your average road kill. Go ahead. My milk is getting warm.

I remember his words today as if they were spoken but a brief moment ago. They were like warm knives cutting cleanly through my salt encrusted rags, shredding them and leaving me naked and painfully exposed. When they reached the hardened callous of my heart; I began to tremble and I watched as the carton of milk in my hands began to shake.

I had to put it down or I was going to crush it.

"You are not alone." he said. "Though you believe it to be so, you are not alone. We don't know you. We don't know what you are running from. But we know this about you. We know that God is with you. This much we both can see. There is a great love surrounding you. Perhaps it is inside of you. But you are shining with it. We want you to take this and buy yourself something to eat with it. We will pray for you. We only wish that there was more that we could give to you; but for now; we think this will be enough."

He held his other hand out to the woman without ever taking his eyes off of me and placed a fifty dollar bill on the table in front of me.

He smiled, squeezed my shoulder with a gentleness I have rarely ever felt, and walked away hand in hand with the old woman toward the door.

I couldn't look up. Instead I whispered "Thank you. To whatever God in heaven that awaits the both of you; from the bottom of my heart I thank you."

In that moment I prayed for them. In that moment of genuine, heartfelt charity; I prayed for them to reap the greatest good, the warmest love, the gentlest of days in the autumn of their lives.

I watched through the window as they made their way to their car. The old man turned to the window where I sat; found me; nodded to me; and smiled.

My eyes were burning as I fought back tears. I managed a brave, manly grimace in return. The old woman paused, looking down at the ground while the old man entered the car and leaned over to open her door. She hesitated as though she had left something behind and then reached for the door of the car.

Then she hesitated again.

Then she turned to me. She was crying shamelessly; bawling like a baby; trying to wave a final, reluctant farewell. And by then, so was I.

49

In my mind's eye it seemed to me that I saw a little girl waving goodbye, and it occurred to me in my own tears that I was not alone. It came to me in that moment that the world was full of wounded people. Each of them carrying in their own lives their own silent pain. Each of them children in a way, giving as best they can to make that nameless pain just a bit more bearable.

I never knew their names. I never knew where they were from or where they were headed, but I remember them. I remember them with a love that they will never begin to imagine possible.

They planted one of many seeds that day that have grown to fruition in the soft and pliant loam of my heart. I knew deep down inside that I would never see them again and never be able to thank them for their gift. They really had no idea what they gave me that day.

But I live in another day, in a new hope, to give small meaning to their selfless act and a testament to their love. Were that the rest of the world should be so kind.

The balance on the scale of my life had been tipped ever so slightly; undetectable yet; but tipped nevertheless in the favor of a saving sarcastic grace said above the paltry offerings of a greasy Formica table in some backwater signpost that pointed like a sucking vortex to the end of my young existence.

The whirlpool of the sewer I called my life pulled at me ever downward still.

The graduation forgotten; forced like a sliver from my consciousness and thrown away; I could focus on more important things. I had in the moment a simple gut wrenching act of kindness to dwell upon, and a beggar's banquet of real food to eat for the first time in many days.

I had money with which to bathe and wash my road worn rags. Nothing is free in a quick rip truck stop on an empty anonymous road.

They cannot know it; but I concede in this moment that it is likely that in the absence of that simple act of kindness, I would not have found the strength or the cunning to go on. I would have found a way to have perished in my solitude.

Hearing Eden's words spill from the mouth of a stranger, call it what you will; was enough in that hour to save me once again from the darkness of my road. It was the awesome, majestic simplicity of that one kind deed that kept my crushing poverty at bay, and in a deeper sense; kept my wounded, crippled spirit alive.

So it comes Eden. As lightening across a darkening sky. I begged of you a kinder, gentler path. But you said that was not to be. You said that orphans would suffer the more and a promise would be kept.

I have suffered the more.

I have deliberated in helpless, sign less silence; torn. With only my heart to guide me in the decisions I must make. I hear in this Orphan Creed a confession of the cruelest kind.

A confession that will leave them crumpled, naked and bleeding; brutalized beyond the realm of any understanding they may hold this day.

It may leave them grieving in breathless, choking, bloody bitterness the innocence it may take from them.

Are they ready to hear a horrific, haunting homily that will coax them gently by the hand and by their heart to wander wide-eyed kicking and screaming in a barren and brutal hopeless hell that I myself have lived to return from?

Because show them I will. If that is to be my destiny. In word and by deed.

That your love and my love does indeed exist.

That it does indeed transcend in laughing, fearless, joy-filled childish exuberance the futile, empty, powerless mediocrity of spite, malice, and maleficent evil both you and I have found and understood in both our worlds.

Chapter Four

Ebron and Sallon approached the dying boy. Both had left the water in the same instant as I did. Tesla and Neva followed a few short minutes later. All us were naked except for a single circlet of gold around each of our wrists.

Ebron is blond. Fine, silken hair cascaded down over his shoulders. He has a rippling scar that stretches in ugly fingers across his chest.

It is a souvenir he brought with him from the equatorial waters off the coast of Chile. He had birthed in the waters you have come to call the Galapagos. He has much to say about the cruelty of men.

Ebron lost his entire family in one hour to Chilean fishing trawlers. His mother had been taken by baited wire line first; and then used as a lure to coax the rest of his pod into the nets.

It is a clever ruse that has killed many of us.

Ebron had heeded his mother's frantic warning and stayed deep. His father had bravely but foolishly approached the trawlers with nine other males and one other female.

Like you; we too, are an emotional creature.

Sometimes our emotions are the end of us. Every one of them wanted in that moment to save Ebron's mother. Had they been able to find the wire, they might have been able to break it. Or maybe even snap it from her mouth.

All of them had been taken in the nets.

Ebron had fled those waters five days later with Sina and three other young females. But only after he surfaced and tracked near the boats once the nets had been drawn and cleared.

A Chilean fisherman had gaffed him in the chest during his single pass alongside the trawler and attempted to draw him onto the deck where Ebron's mother and father both lay gutted and dead. The others who had attempted to rescue Ebron's mother in the first had fared no better.

The Chilean fisherman had laughed viciously as he hauled on the gaff, calling Ebron "un tontito," and yelled to his shipmates for help to drag the wounded dolphin into the boat.

In Spanish, "un tontito" means "silly one" or "fool."

Ebron was no fool.

His struggle on the end of the gaff had earned him the wound and the scar, and a lingering memory of the sight of the dead bodies of his mother and father on the deck of the trawler; but it had also saved him his life.

Ebron's circle lost 5,000 that year.

Their bodies were cut into pieces and used as crab bait.

Sina had led Ebron and three younger females first south along the coast, and then east through the Drake, and then north around the Horn. One of the weaker females perished of the bitter cold in that journey. They rested with an Ur pod for a year in the island waters of the Corlin reach before continuing on.

Then they had taken the current north and sought the call.

Another of the young females was taken by a Portugese harpoon.

It was near the mouth of the great river you call the Amazon. Sina had perished by rifle shot trying to rescue her. Becca was the only female to survive the journey into the Sargasso Sea with Ebron.

Sallon came from the Appa Sea near the old places. He is older than Ebron by two hundred years and showed the signs of grey in his hair that marked a life of gentle wisdom.

His entire pod had been taken, including his mother and father; by tuna fishers in one afternoon five years earlier. He had watched as the drowned bodies of his parents were first cleared of the nets and then thrown over the side of the vessel with the rest of the unwanted dead.

The water had been too deep to retrieve them, but he was alone anyway. He had circled the spot for seven days keening for them, and then he fled in mindless grief southward to the call.

Tesla is the orphan of Nerri and Pim. Her mother and father had been taken by tuna fishers as well in the cooler waters of the northern seas. She had wandered, lost and grieving to the range two short years ago. She is the only survivor of her pod. Tesla is taller by a hand than Ebron and Sallon and greatly fair of face. Her hair is the color of a starless night.

Tesla is the only virgin among us.

Neva is my youngest sister by a century. Mara had come in the half time between my birth. After Neva was born, there would be no more from our line. Jodan and Ama; my father and mother; disappeared one night to frolic; but had never returned.

Our pod had searched for them for months but we found no sign of them. We encountered long nets in our search and we assumed the worst had happened. Ama had been Keeper of Our Way. On her death; it fell to me.

In human stature, Neva is blond like Ebron, only her hair is coarser, and braided into an intricate weave which falls to her hips. Her eyes betray the difference of ages between her and I and shows a wisdom beyond her years. She smiles. Her eyes smile. Her heart smiles. She is a smile. But she is not smiling now. She is grieving the death of her sister Mara.

I have never seen my sister weep in human form. It is a sadness I have never known and never wish to know again; to see her weep though she smiles.

I knelt beside the boy and brushed the sand from his face. I could tell he was not long for this world. I whispered into his ear that I was there. I think he heard me. He opened his eyes briefly.

To be honest, I was a bit startled; because it seemed as though he recognized me. And then he closed his eyes and drifted away.

Ebron swooped the boy up like a gull sweeping a minnow. There was no weight to this human form in Ebron's arms. We were all unfamiliar with our human bodies. It has been many centuries since we have worn them.

Seeing each of them walk upright for the first time took my breath away. Walking upright upon land myself was a broken promise. It was a forbidden taboo I knew would harvest unknown consequences.

All I could hope for was a forgiveness in the purity of our motives.

I love them.

Standing there in the darkness under the starlit sky with heaven as my witness; I loved them. Ebron, Neva, Tesla, Sallon. They were my family now. I wondered what punishment we had invited for this most egregious of crimes we had in this act committed.

Few had dared to break this promise.

And those few who had; paid for that breaking with their lives.

What made the matter worse is that I am Keeper of Our Way. I should; knowing better than any of them; of all of them; chosen otherwise.

I looked out over the silence of the lagoon and the many hundreds of my brethren waiting there; watching us; and traced my toes thru the fine wet of the sand.

The tears on my face were a wonder to me. It is all a wonder to me. And it is a living grief to me to know the peril in which they live each day. It was not intended to be this way.

"Go now." I whispered to them. "Go in peace. Be safe. Remember us. Remember Mara, my sister. Know that we love you. Go."

The lagoon exploded with life as my kindred; my orphaned brothers and sisters from another time and place; my dwindling beloved who had been respectfully and patiently waiting in the calm darkness all leapt in unison from the depths in one final salute to my whispered words. Becca fled our seeming madness with them.

Somehow I knew in that darkness that everything would find its reason.

Neva took my hand, tugged gently, and I turned from the lagoon and followed slowly behind as Tesla led Ebron and Sallon to the edge of the jungle canopy.

She stopped, closed her eyes, and gracefully raised her arms above her head. I remember thinking how beautiful she looked in her human form.

In the darkness I could see the curves of her silhouette. I could see the firm rise of her breasts; the tight sinew of her calves; the soft edge of her belly against the sharp relief of the black jungle interior. I dimly remembered what it was to be a woman. I remembered the sensuous feeling of being alive in human form. I remembered how seductive it had been.

I remembered in that moment the promises we had made and the reasons we had made them. I knew in that moment the risks we were taking.

I broke a promise. How will I redeem myself? Is it even possible?

Those questions and many others would have to wait.

Tesla crossed her wrists and touched the golden bracelets together and laid open a hidden path into the interior of the trees.

Silence followed us into the foliage.

We walked noiselessly through the lush, crowded copse of palms until we came to a clearing which opened into a circle sixty feet in diameter. My mother had told me of this place, and her mother before her. It had been passed down from one generation to the next. There was no question of its existence. There was no doubt in our minds. Each of us had been here; or a place similar to it; before.

Tesla repeated the mute gesture once again and opened her eyes as the ground on which we stood suddenly began to vibrate.

The center of the clearing began to heave and push slowly and quietly upwards, folding the accumulated humus of the luxuriant tropical garden slowly over and upon itself.

From within the center of the mound rose a large stone dais portaled on the four cardinal points of the compass with heavy, hewn coral doors. The roof of the dais was covered with centuries of debris.

"Had it had been that long?" I thought.

I will be remembered for breaking the promise. This will be my legacy. I won't be remembered for saving the life of this human child. I will be remembered for condemning my companions and breaking a promise that had been kept by my mother, and her mother before her, and her mother before her.

What have I done?

Set into the center of each door was a circle of gold similar to the one each of us wore on our wrists, only much larger and thicker. Tesla stepped up to the north portal and touched her wrist to the ring and stepped back.

The door thudded in the silence and began a slow, grating, lumbering retraction that bespoke the many centuries it had lain closed to the outside world. I wondered if it was as we had left it when we fled. I wondered if anything had survived the centuries of our absence and neglect.

When the grating stopped, the silence fell over us like an accusation and a warm light poured out from the open interior. It seemed to be bathing Tesla's naked human form. She was beautiful. Tesla basked in this warm, beautiful light under a starlit sky.

I wished the boy was conscious so he could see this.

I wished he was awake so I could tell him what this was going to cost us.

Tesla stepped into the light and disappeared. Ebron and Sallon followed Tesla into the light. I paused for a moment. There was no going back now.

It was too late. It is too late for many things. But it is not too late for some things. The orphaned child will tell you this. He will tell you what it is too late for.

I am not sorry for saving his life.

I could have let him die. I would have felt sorrow for that.

I could feel Neva behind me. Her thoughts were a gentle caress in the turmoil I was feeling in that moment. I could not have asked for a greater friend or a more loyal companion in this task. She has been all of these.

What future lies ahead for us? What horizon will we find in this breaking of an agreement we made so long ago with the Great Ocean?

Neva led me into the light and I said a whispered goodbye to the night.

The door rumbled shut behind us as we made our way down a long stairwell carved into the coral. The steps had been worn smooth by human feet thousands of years earlier. A narrow gantry led into a cavernous hall carved under the coral and into the granite mantle of the earth itself.

It all seemed vaguely familiar to me; as if I had been away for a very long time and was just now remembering that I once had lived here. My mother had spoken to me of this place.

This was my remembrance. This was my inheritance. I look back on it now and I realize that everything happens for a reason.

We may not understand in the moment what that reason is; but nothing occurs in the Great Ocean without a cause or a purpose to it. My task now would be to give some purpose or meaning to this broken promise.

The boy would live or every consequence we would suffer for my decision would be for naught.

It was enough for me to know that our purpose was pure and our motives were true.

Sallon approached Neva and I. He was carrying robes and sandals.

The soft light which permeated through the rock illuminated everything but it gave no warmth to the dry cool of this place. We were becoming human very quickly again.

It would not be long before we began to suffer as humans do. It would not be long before we became again much as humans are.

Tesla would not remain a virgin in this place were we to remain naked for very long. Ebron and Sallon were both wonderful frolics.

I had known and enjoyed both of them many times. They would both leap at the pleasure of Tesla. But that would need to wait.

Ebron had placed the boy on the center stone. Tesla had already begun her prayers. She would need all of us if the boy were to survive. We joined her in the circle. Sallon was to my left. Neva was on my right. When Sallon took my hand, I remembered why I loved him as much as I did.

He reminded me of my father.

I wondered in that moment if my father would have approved of my decisions.

Sallon had known my father, Jodan well. The two of them had tangled over my mother, Ama; with Jodan winning her final approval. To think that Sallon could have been my father was a warm thought that comforted me. Sallon's proud look and his warm touch reassured me that my father would have approved of the course that had led us here. I was Keeper of Our Way. I had made the only choice there was to make. Sallon approved or he would not be standing here with me.

Ebron smiled as I thought these thoughts. He was always eavesdropping on me. I loved him so much. He had known my father, too.

I will not share with you the prayer we made in that circle. It is a private thing among our species.

The only way to know it is to be as we are. The boy knows it. He knows our Origin. He knows to Whom we prayed. He knows his Origin. He knows the Prayer to Whom we prayed.

The center stone radiated with warmth as we turned our hearts to the boy. A soft golden Light began to surround him. We are born from this Light. We are made of this Light. We are healed by this Light. We serve this Light. We serve the Light.

When he opened his eyes; the boy was gently blinded by this Light. It was better that he should hear and feel us first before he saw us.

It was I who broke the circle and touched him first.

The light slowly fell away as Ebron and Tesla touched him. Neva and Sallon both reached for him as the light finally dimmed to nothingness.

"You are healed, young one." were the only words he heard in his mind.

They were spoken by my voice. It was the kindest thing I could do. They were felt by him more than they were heard by us.

This is one of many gifts that we have that we have made to him. His language and ours would have been an impossible barrier for him to overcome. The trauma of his awakening deaf to our words in this place would have done him more harm than good had we not made it to him.

We cannot undo it. We cannot undo any of it. He must learn to live with this gift. Just as he must learn to live with the many others we have made to him. But not all gifts are a blessing. Nor are all blessings a gift. Some may be a curse. So we have come to learn; and so too has he come to discover.

We stepped back and let him sit up. He was immediately aware and ashamed of his nakedness; but Sallon had anticipated this and humbly offered him a robe. He took it hesitantly.

We could sense his confusion and fear. But we also sensed that he knew we meant him no harm.

I knew he was having a difficult time making a connection between the events of his most recent memory and the events of the moment. I could hear his thoughts clearly now and I was learning a great deal about him; even though he was completely unaware of this.

In the many hours that I had taken to bring him to the lagoon; I had not devoted any energy at all to learning anything about him. The immediacy of the moment had not allowed for it.

I had the leisure now to read him.

I knew the others were reading him as well.

We kept our thoughts from him until he collected his own. The sound of his own voice frightened him when he spoke. It echoed in the emptiness of the hall. He stopped speaking as quickly as he began.

There was a frantic quality to him; to his thoughts. He was doing a fair job of concealing it. But his thoughts were impossible to conceal. He remembered throwing the rifle into the ocean. He remembered my approach. But he didn't remember much after that. He remembered the cook shooting Mara.

But he didn't know who we were or that Mara was my sister.

This was going to be more difficult than I had imagined.

How was I going to explain our presence in his world without betraying my own?

Maybe I should have left him to die. I was beginning to realize why we were only obligated to bring human beings to land. I was beginning to realize why we were forbidden to interfere beyond the shore. Ebron came to my rescue and again; I was struck by the depth of his love; now most especially; in light of Ebron's loss.

Ebron stepped slowly closer to the boy and let his robe slip to the floor.

The boy looked at him.

He saw Ebron's scar and then a quizzical look crossed his face. I was reading his thoughts as he noted that Ebron appeared to be circumcised... but no...that's impossible. The boy was smart. He was observant.

Tesla took the cue from Ebron. She made the boy blush as she dropped her robe. He averted his eyes at first. He was both shy and a virgin. His erection was immediate and obvious to everybody. But somehow he knew that we wanted him to look.

Sallon dropped his robe next and the boy confirmed his suspicion. Sallon didn't have one either. Neva and I dropped our robes together. It was unanimous.

None of us had navels. The only one in the hall with a belly button was the boy.

We all smiled together. He looked at Tesla and she nodded. I knew in that instant that his fear was gone. Tesla had broken through. She had made contact with him. He was communicating with her.

Tesla confirmed it by stepping back up to the center stone; reaching under the robe on the boy's lap; and gently squeezing his erection. His beet red blush suggested that he had indeed healed completely. The boy instantly ejaculated into Tesla's hand. She smiled at him and withdrew; picked up her robe; and took his hand and helped him down from the center stone.

We followed them out into the warm tropical night.

Tesla led the boy to the beach. The quarter moon was high in the sky and the horizon was filled with stars. The lagoon was silent except for the sound of the waves softly lapping at the sand.

Tesla lost her human virginity that night.

Each of us did.

Chapter Five

"I am the vagrant son. The son of a bitch. The little wretch."
"I will become random acts of mindless violence. A promise kept."

I get to watch it all again. From my heart, I would have it no other way. Each moment is real for me in my memory. And now it is alive. But I am not alone. I was never alone. I have Eden's whispered voice to comfort me in this lonely road before me. I am not alone in it as I was when first I wandered there.

It is almost funny.

I look back and I can see him. I knew him better than anybody else in the world. Its like he still lives in my moments. He does. But he wasn't even a man in most of them.

I was just fifteen when the hardest turns were taken. I hadn't even begun to shave yet. I didn't talk much either. I was a quiet type. A loner. Most orphans and runaways are. It was run or hang to me. Nothing more. Nothing less. It was that simple.

I've seen and known lots of them; and buried a few of them; my younger brother among them.

Many of us end up on a stainless steel table at some hospital morgue somewhere with a toe tag that says Juvenile John or Jane Doe, but all of us were somebody's child.

Some of us are in prison.

Many of us are dead.

Miami was full of them. Every city that I wandered had its share of them.

Human beings have a lot to be ashamed about. Forcing their children onto the streets and into prostitution, starvation, or addiction are just a few of the things they will have difficulty explaining to their maker when they make the pearly gates. If that's where they go at all.

Believe me; if animals did to themselves what we do to ourselves; the planet wouldn't be anywhere near as crowded as it is. It would be a barren, silent, empty place.

You couldn't miss these children even if you tried. Which really means that you have to look the other way. That implies that you do see them and that you don't really care. It means that they don't really matter.

All you have to do is troll the boulevards at night or hit the gay bars or heroin shooting galleries to find them.

Most of them; not all of them; spend a brief stint in one or the other; or both of them before they die.

If I'd known beforehand where and to what I was headed, I would have tied my hands behind my back before I jumped with that rope around my neck.

There was no way I could have known I was jumping from the frying pan into the fire.

I still had the rope burns on my neck when I made it there.

I wasn't much different than any of the other runaways I suppose.

I think the stark reality of it all finally hit me a couple of days after I arrived in Miami. I was sitting in this huge, empty yard where they stage all kinds of stuff that's headed for export to some poorer undeveloped country that can't either feed itself or build itself. The yard kind of reminded me of me at the time. Empty. Deserted. Lifeless.

It was one of the funniest thing I ever saw. Or maybe it wasn't so funny.

I just thought it was at the time.

There I was sitting there inside the fence of this huge yard, picking up handfuls of dusty coral crusher run and pouring them out into neat little piles. Like a five year old sitting in a giant sand box making little mountains as he played.

But I was crying. The tears and the dust made these bright red streaks down my face. I was praying furiously.

Just about every kid who ever ends up on the street learns to pray at one point or another. Sometimes they learn to pray just before the moment of their death. But by then it is usually too late. Most of them don't know how to pray or who or what they are praying to or what they are praying for.

I was one of those.

It was funny.

I can hear me now.

I was saying "Please God. If there is a God." And every now and then I would throw in a "Sir" for good measure almost as if in the off chance that there was a God; I didn't want to take the chance of pissing him off anymore than I already had.

It was comical.

That kind of solidified it for me.

I was wondering how it was all going to turn out.

I had watched the sunrise that morning. I had slept in a huge concrete sewer tile that had been stacked in the yard six high. There had been hundreds of them here, maybe thousands of them here in the morning waiting to be shipped to El Guatemala or somewhere.

I had left everything I owned wrapped neatly in a green laundry bag that I had carried south with me in the tile as I left in the morning in search of work. The only change of clothes I had were in it. What few cherished personal mementoes of my life before I was orphaned were in it. The only photograph I had of my mother was in it. I thought it would be safe.

I had walked around Miami for a full two days before I got the idea that the sewer tiles might be a good place to hole up for a while. I had taken refuge in the Greyhound Bus station, but I was beginning to get looks from the people who worked there.

You can only sleep in the chairs for a while before you have to buy a ticket and get on a bus or move on.

"Its called loitering, son."

"I'm not your son..... Dad."

Oops. Poisoned that well.

Some runaways give up after about a day or two. They turn themselves into the police or a church or something and then they go home and apologize to their parents and do extra homework or chores or something.

Some of them intentionally commit a crime to get arrested; figuring that Juvenile Hall is better than the abuse they had in foster care. At least in Juvenile Hall you get three hots and a cot. Juvie ain't so bad. A few fights. But you eat on a regular basis.

Some of them find their way to the Salvation Army or the homeless shelters where they can scrounge a few tasteless "baked in a barrel" meals.

They sleep in the billets until some old, toothless pervert gropes or fondles them in the middle of the night, and then they turn themselves over.

Some of them become immediate prey to the many and diverse predators who have learned to spot and then feed upon them.

For me, it was all or nothing. I had a rope with my name on it waiting for me. It was learn the dance or drop and swing.

That's why it was so funny.

When I left the five star concrete sewer tile to explore the city and look for work that morning; I left that little green laundry bag with everything I had managed to bring with me right smack dab in the center of the highest one I could climb.

It was probably the first one that they loaded onto a ship. It was probably the last one that was taken off the ship. Some lucky bum in South America found everything I owned neatly folded in that little green bag.

I wondered what he thought of that? I wonder what he thought of the picture of my mom? I wonder...

I thought it would be safe there. It was. Only I would never see it again.

I remember spending thirty cents of the last sixty-five cents I had when I got to Miami to buy the Herald. I thumbed through the help-wanted ads but I was immediately and completely overwhelmed by the street addresses and sheer enormity of my total poverty.

I used the last thirty-five cents I had to purchase a cup of rancid Cuban coffee. I may not have been going anywhere fast; but I was going to be wide awake when I got there.

I would guess I walked twelve, maybe fifteen miles that day. Circles mostly. Block after endless block. Little Havana mostly. Between the heat of the sub-tropical day and the exertion of the endless walk; the dehydration and hunger; I lost maybe three or four pounds easily.

I was a bean pole to begin with.

Gaunt was a word that comes to mind.

Half of the city's beggars hit me up for change that day.

"Sorry man. If I had it, I'd share it."

By the end of the day I had it down pat.

In a way it was like a skip on an old vinyl record playing a really bad tune. Some of the winos and stew bums were just sitting there waiting for death to take them.

I'm glad I was broke. I would have given what money I had away.

There is something vividly compelling about a wretched, filthy old man sitting in a puddle of his own urine asking for enough money to buy a bottle of Mogen David 20 20.

Of course it begs the question; "Whose urine would he be sitting in other than his own?" Don't ask.

I think I noticed it on the corner of Northeast 2nd Avenue and 6th Street. A lot happened to me on that corner. But I think the actual shock of it hit me like a brick about the third or fourth step after I turned that corner.

My life has been like that. One second I'm bee-bopping along, just breathing, and then WHAM! Life just reaches out and takes your breath away. That's' what it was. I have to say the sight was breathtaking.

I think I said something like, "You got to be kidding me."

If you look east from that corner; you can see Biscayne Bay. If you look over to the right; there's Dodge Island and the old Miami Marina and Government Cut blowing the channel eastward out on to the Atlantic. On the left as you look, there's MacArthur Causeway heading out to Miami Beach.

My heart skipped a beat and my pace picked up a little bit. By the time I hit Biscayne Boulevard two blocks away, I was moving. As tired as I was after my little day hike; I was running like a rabbit with a dog on his ass.

I scaled the chainlink fence which bordered the yard in two strides and dropped into the crusher run and just stood there. I looked over my shoulder at this huge bleaching sign of a little girl with a tiny terrier pulling her bikini bottom down just a little. It was an old Coppertone ad from ages ago painted on the side of one of Miami's old hotels. She was my only witness.

Her and the universe.

I just stood there like a Yosemite Sam character in a Bugs Bunny Cartoon wondering how running down here was supposed to make the mirage disappear or something.

I couldn't help myself. I had to laugh.

Somebody done gone and stole about two bejillion sewer tiles.

There I was standing there in this huge yard with my arms all akimbo; looking around, up, down, like maybe they were hidden under something somewhere.

Alright, who done it? Where'd they go. Cough them up; my stuff was in them. The jokes over. Stop kidding around.

"Ain't no joke, kid." I whispered to myself. "This ain't no joke."

I was laughing so hard I almost peed myself.

So what are you going to do now? You didn't figure on this, did you? Are you just going to stand there and laugh? Are you just going to sit there and cry? Huh? Huh? Go ahead, kid. Might as well get it over with while nobody is watching. Nobody but that little girl up there on that building and she don't really give no never mind. How would it look?

Some tough guy you are. It didn't hurt that much. Suck it up. Suck everything up.

You're already dead. You just don't know it yet.

I said it aloud.

I heard myself say it.

I looked up when I said it and threw another handful of crusher run into the neat little piles I had made. I stood up and looked around, worried that somebody might have seen me crying; or worse; heard me say what I had said.

There isn't anything more beautiful than a tropical sunset.

Well; that isn't necessarily true. But at that moment, the sun was setting. My sun was setting. My concrete bed; my shelter for the night; along with everything I owned in the world; was on a cruise somewhere in the Caribbean.

After the sun's corona had blazed it's way across the horizon; I dusted myself off and for reasons still unknown to me, pointed myself in the general direction of Dodge Island and started trudging toward it. It was getting dark.

Hunger was biting at me. My throat was parched. My feet hurt. I was a mess. I was penniless. I wondered how much longer I would last. The only good thing, if there was one; was that I no longer had anything to carry.

Dodge Island was about two miles away. I climbed back over the fence and headed south along the boulevard. I could see the lights of the Empress and the Princess slowly lighting up as darkness fell. They were my beacon as I walked.

They were the seed of an idea which began to form in my mind.

I could see cruise ships docked the length of the island. Maybe. Just maybe. The worst they could say was no. That was a mistake.

All I had to do was get there.

The possibilities seemed endless as I walked.

What I came to call The Law of Proportion was coming into play.

How bad could it get?

Maybe one of those cruise ships needed a deck hand or a mess boy. Working on a cruise ship wouldn't be so bad. They feed you. You have a place to sleep. That's the ticket. I'll get a job on a cruise ship!

I'll travel the Caribbean.

"Sure you will. Uh huh. You'll marry the Captain's daughter and pretty soon everybody will be working for you. Yeah. Sure."

"Hey kid. Where are you headed?"

The car was a big old Cadillac. It was a sun faded gold with a paunchy, balding, fiftyish, older man wearing a wife beater t-shirt leaning over the seat as the power window slowly hummed down.

I answered without thinking.

Between the weary hunger and being lost in thought, my guard was down.

"Over to the cruise ships."

Uh huh. Here we go. Didn't your mother ever teach you not to talk to strangers, kid?

"Here, get in. I'll give you a ride."

"Jeez, thanks Mister. But it's a nice night, and it isn't far. Thanks. But I think I'll walk."

The guy in the car was crafty. He been here before. This wasn't anything new for him. He'd polished this line like a silver serving fork.

"Hey. Listen kid. It isn't any of my business; but you look like you could use some money. Are you new around here? Would you like something to eat?"

He's fishing. That's count them...one, two, three hooks. Will you bite?

Yeah. I'm hungry. I haven't eaten in days. Let me see. The last thing I had to eat was a sandwich. I had used a dollar to buy a loaf of bread and an orange drink. I shoplifted the lunch meat. Then I made myself a little picnic while I fed the pigeons what bread I couldn't stuff myself with.

SO.... the answer is..... Yeah. I'm hungry. Does it show?

New around here? Does that show too? No. I'm not new. I'm old. In fact, I'm guessing now that what you're thinking of hoping of doing with me is probably against the law given the fact that I haven't reached the age of legal consent yet. So the answer to that question is ...is...No.

"Don't listen to him. Keep walking. Don't stop.'

"He likes young boys and he knows who and what you are. He's been here before and done this before. Keep moving."

My internal monologue was screaming now. "He wants to diddle you!"

"Hey kid, would you like to make a quick twenty bucks?"

Whoa! Now we were talking real money. Twenty bucks. What would you do for twenty bucks if you hadn't eaten in days? What would you do for twenty bucks if you hadn't eaten in days; had no place to live; no job; and knew absolutely no one in a dark city that was getting darker by the minute?

What I couldn't do with twenty bucks.

I could get something to eat. Something sweet, like a donut; or Chinese food maybe. Find a hostel and take a shower. How bad would it be? When was the last time I bathed? Lets see....

Today is Wednesday? I left on Friday? Five days? Maybe as many meals? Twenty bucks, huh. And what do I get for door number two?

Like I didn't know already.

But now I got a choice in the matter.

Where before I never did.

"No way, buddy. Go fuck yourself!"

I laughed at him as he tried to burn rubber in his decrepit old caddy. He was shouting out the window "Go ahead and starve you little punk. You'd have loved it!"

"Ya. In your dreams. You fucking weirdo! I'd RATHER STARVE!"

I probably would at this rate. Things were just getting better and better.

"Snappy comeback, kid."

"So how do you like Miami, kid?"

"We call it the land of the Newly Weds, and the Nearly Deads. Didja just get married, kid? Oh really? So where is your lovely bride?"

I never made it to the cruise ships.

I wasn't on Dodge Island five minutes before they had the lights on me.

Miami is one of those ports of entry for all kinds of interesting things. It sees its share of illegal drugs, aliens, and all sorts of contraband.

The main port is heavily patrolled and I stuck out like a two dollar whore at a Sunday bake sale.

I didn't know how anything worked in the larger world at that point but I was a quick study. Years of quiet observation in the hostile world of foster care had taught me to shut my mouth and listen and watch.

I learned a lot about human nature by watching the drama of human ego unfold in living technicolor before my eyes. Many were the times I wore the reminders of those episodes in the hazy colors of black and blue.

The two officers from the Customs Patrol that halted my exploration of Dodge Island were surprised that I spoke English. I gave them a fake I.D. that I had stolen from the school commissary and forged in the library. It said I was 18. That was a lie. I fed them a rehearsed line that I had graduated High School the previous June and had come south looking for work. It was partly true.

I was looking for work.

I would have done anything at that point. I was so hungry. And now it appeared as though I was about to be found out.

They passed the I.D. back and forth between themselves and looked me up and down. One of them looked at the I.D. and then gave me a hard look, and something inside me thought, "Damn! He knows."

He asked me to get in the back of the patrol car. When he closed the door behind me I noticed there were no door handles or knobs to roll the windows down.

"Guess what kid?"

"You should have taken the first ride that was offered to you. You know. The one from the guy who looked like he could suck the dimples off a golf ball? The fucking you would have taken in that ride wouldn't have been any where near as bad as the one it looks like you're about to get in this one."

The Customs building on Dodge Island was like a small fortress, complete with armed sentries and cells and a booking room.

I'm busted. Might as well relax and take the beating. How long can it last? Beatings hurt more and the injuries linger longer when you tense up. It has something to do with muscle rigidity. I learned that a long time ago.

I figured I was headed straight to the booking room. Fingerprints first; photographing, name, date of birth, place of birth, prior arrest record; all that stuff.

Then a strip search; cavity search; and a holding cell while they ran my prints. That would take a day or so. Maybe they'll feed me. Probably not.

They brought me to their lunch room and sat me down.

I didn't know what to say. I was dumbfounded.

I told them I was staying at the bus station until I found a place to live and some kind of job. I realized the break I was getting and I swear I didn't want to lie to them, but I didn't want to be found out either. They gave me my I.D. back.

One of them went to the refrigerator in the lunch room and gave me half of his lunch. We talked as I ate. I think they knew I was lying. But I think they knew I was running from something really ugly too.

They weren't in any position to change my life.

They knew it and they knew I knew it.

So they let me eat and then they let me go.

They gave me a ride to the bridge that led back to the boulevard. One of them gave me his business card and a folded twenty dollar bill. He told me to give him a call in the morning and he would see what he could do about finding me a job on the dock.

As I walked back to the bus station I deliberated the half sandwich he had given me. It was turkey on wheat bread, with lettuce and mayo. I couldn't trust him to leave it at that. There would be questions that I couldn't answer if I went back. I would be found out. I was absolutely certain someone, somewhere, was looking for me. If for no other reason than to inflict punishment on me for stepping outside the box.

I wasn't going back. I had made up my mind. I would die first.

I carried his card in my wallet as a reminder of his kindness.

I lost it the day Hanz threw me overboard.

I wonder at times what would have become of me if I had called him the next day. So much in my life has ridden and turned on the fall of a dime in a pay phone; a call I made or didn't make.

I remember that Customs Officer today. I thank him for his kindness and for that sandwich that took the hunger from my belly for just a little while.

I thank him for a future he offered me. I wish I could tell him that the future he envisioned for me that night was one that was never meant for me to have. But I thank him. I thank him for a spontaneous charity as well. I thank the universe for hearing my prayer in the dust of that empty yard and leading me to him.

Twenty bucks. What I did with twenty bucks. I took my sneaker off, pulled the nylon liner out of it; tucked the twenty dollar bill under it and replaced the liner. Now I had money in the bank. I was good to go.

There is absolutely nothing quite like the few hours in the wee stretch of the early morning; those grainy, fuzzy hours between 2 and 5 AM. Spend them shooing away beggars and weirdos in a tacky, grimy bus station that is brighter in the fluorescent lighting than a supernova.

Use them to contemplate and warp one's sense and perception of loss.

Sit in a hard plastic chair with a miniature T.V. bolted to it that takes quarters and plays one channel in 15 minute increments. Smell yourself.

You'll get a picture, but you won't be able to quite tune it in.

It wasn't a comedy. It was a dramedy. Stay tuned campers.

Quarters. My kingdom for a quarter.

"Hey Mister! Can you spare a quarter so I can watch T.V.? I don't want to buy a bottle of wine. I just want to watch fifteen minutes of T.V. I haven't had a bath in a week and this weather really makes me sweat, and now I don't have a change of clothes because they decided to vacation in El Guatemala by sewer tile; but like; could I bum a quarter so I can watch fifteen minutes of television?"

I really miss television.

Hey Mister. Where are you going? Hey Mister?

Hey buddy? Have you got a quarter you can spare?

What a maroon! I've been marooned! I'm gonna send ya to the moon! Alice! Right to the moon!

"Getting a little punchy, kid?"

"No sleepy?"

"Miss that nice warm bed you used to have just a few thousand miles ago?"

"Better get your head out of your butt, buddy."

Hey butt buddy! Can you spare a quarter?

Not in a million years, man. Not on your life. How many quarters would it take to buy that television bolted to your chair. Hey, the chair is bolted to the floor. Hey, I'm bolted to this chair. About one more quarter than you have to spare.

Maybe there's a quarter in the change compartments in those pay phones over there? Hey. Yeah. Maybe. Hey.

"Go check it."

"Operator. May I help you, sir?"

Hey; she called you "sir." Things are really looking up.

I want to place a long distance collect phone call.

A very heavy pause. It weighed about as much as a two ton sewer tile.

"I really love you, Tony. You are the best friend I ever had. I will always love you. Live a good life. Don't ever forget me."

The click as I hung up the phone was like a hammer pulling back, cocked, loaded. Then a boom that echoed through the bus station as I gently put the phone back down on the receiver.

It was like a gun going off.

What a miserable sight. He's cracking like Humpty Dumpty. And all the king's horses and all the king's men ain't gonna be putting this boy together again.

Yeah. I was crying again. And I really didn't give a rat's ass at that point who saw me. Like maybe one of the winos in the audience was going to come up to me at that point; put his arm around me in a warm hug; and say "Hey man; don't cry; I love you, dude. Here, drink some of this; it'll make you feel better."

Uh huh. It was time to meet the world again. I'd loitered long enough.

I am confused now. It is quiet in my mind. It is still. The voice of Eden is silent like the street of that morning. All of them whom I loved in that day are dead or waiting for me. They are my friends.

I love them still.

I can feel the humid heat of the Miami morning. I can taste the salt in the breeze blowing in from the Atlantic ocean. I can smell the stench of urine from the winos who have relieved themselves against the outside wall of the bus station. I can smell the sweet attar of Night Train, Thunderbird, and Mogen David; the slow poisons of desperate, dying men whose lives are finished in this fly trap of humanity.

I saw him in his cap and gown on his graduation day. I never expected to see him again. I called him because I loved him. He saw me; a shining ghoul in my beautiful lying crushed denim three piece Levi suit. We never spoke. I never saw or heard from him again. He was my best friend. A childhood companion who watched as my life began a slow unravel that no one could stop.

I know he loved me. I cannot help but feel I betrayed that love by running. His parents would have helped me I think. I never asked. I often wonder what became of him.

I hate myself as I stand there in that empty morning street. I hate it. I can see the pigeons flocking; picking from the filthy curbs. Nothing is moving except them and the creeping shame I feel in something crawling over and around me like some slithering reptile I cannot shake. I cannot reach him. He runs.

I cannot see his steps through his tears. It is as if he is dead. Alive but dead. Growing colder by the moment.

I was so lonely. I was so hungry. My pain was a raw nerve that throbbed as I walked up and down the block outside the station.

It blotted out every other possible thing I could feel.

Another day had thrust itself upon me.

It wasn't what I wanted.

Be careful what you wish for.

I had been betrayed by people I had trusted and cared about.

Such is innocence. It would happen over and over again. Until I became like everybody else on the planet. Smiling, treacherous, and cruel.

I was cooked. The chances were pretty good that if today was as good as yesterday was; I'd be done by nightfall. I'd be finished by the setting of the sun. Maybe I'd be performing one of the Sutras on somebody's penis after all. It didn't look good.

I was fried. I stood on the sidewalk outside of the bus station for a few minutes and then that arm went up again.

"Jeez kid, you sure do cry an awful lot. What are you, lonely or something?"

"Get a friggin goldfish or something, would you?"

Between the lack of sleep and a metabolism that was in slow melt down, I was anybody's bet.

Walking back down to Dodge Island was definitely out. I had resolved in the early morning deliberation that there were just too many risks to take with a kind Customs Officer who would most certainly be asking even more questions this morning. That was a good idea. Return to the scene of the crime. Lying to a sworn officer of the law. Start with that.

Make an even bigger target of myself. Dumb, dumb, dumb.

I appreciated his kindness and generosity in a way he can't possibly know; but there was no way I could ever take him up on his offer. Maybe?

No! Move kid. Think while you walk. You think good on your feet. You always have. Think while you move. Something will come to you. You have all day to figure out what you are going to do. You have money in the bank. You can always find a nice policeman and give yourself up and go home and do lots of extra homework or something. Or hang.

A lot of them had. Just how bad was it? Who was I? Where did I come from? What drove me here? Where and how did he get that scar? Or that one?

These are the questions they asked when a kid was laying on the stainless steel table with his blood draining out the hole at the end.

"Where do you think he came from doctor?"

"I don't know. The police report said he was robbed and raped before he was killed. Note the cause of death: Homicide. Manner: Strangulation. Verify the rape; send the semen samples to the lab for cross reference and storage and mark the file Juvenile John Doe. Estimate his age at late fourteen...early fifteen."

"It's so sad. This is the third Juvenile we've had this week. And he's such a handsome boy. I have a boy his age at home. I think I want to cry."

"Mary. Don't go there. The least we can do is treat him decently here. He's never been fingerprinted and he had no identification on him. The police will circulate his photograph through the homeless shelters and hope for a hit, but until then, we'll file his autopsy with the others."

So how would they describe me?

"You're a good for nothing little lying fuck! You can't be trusted and you don't deserve this family! We ought to send you back to where you belong and let someone else worry about you!"

"We tried to be nice to you and you accuse us of this? Of all the gratitude! We don't love you! We never did! You're sick, boy! Something just isn't right about you! I ought to give you a what for just for opening that little pie hole of yours! You make me sick!"

"Who the fuck do you think you are?"

"You won't ever be nothing. I wouldn't be surprised if you don't end up in prison or worse! That's what you deserve! Get out of my sight before I lose my temper and do something we both are going to regret! Go on! Get out you slimy little whining bastard weasel fuck! Get out!"

Or something like that.

"Are you ready Mary? Male. Caucasian. Approximate age; fourteen, fifteen, maybe sixteen years old. Dirty blond hair cut short and trim. Approximate height; seventy two inches. Fair skin. Weight; 150 pounds. Lets see. Hmmnn. Hazel eyes. Full set of teeth, some have been filled. Have dental make a record and an impression. No tattoos. He's been beaten before. Blunt trauma scars on right shoulder. Right cheek. Right distal eye socket. Left cheek. Left wrist broken. Left middle finger broken and healed poorly. That should do."

Too bad he couldn't see inside.

Too bad I couldn't see inside.

I look there today. It was dark and angry in there.

A rage was growing in there. Red. Glowing under a blanket of fury that would one day leap in blinding brilliance out into the world.

I wanted someone; anyone; just to love me. Just love me. Please God. Just love me. Hold me. I have a heart. What did I do? Who did I hurt? TELL ME!

Dear God in heaven. Sir. If there is one. Please. Just tell me. What did I do... who did I hurt to deserve this?

Chapter Six

Sallon departed us on the dawn. I am so angry and so sad on the one; and so touched and so moved on the other. The boy will never really truly know what this wise, gentle, harmless soul sacrificed in this act. I will meet Sallon one day again and frolic with him in an ocean far greater than the one I have come to know and love on this planet in this here and now.

It was such a selfless gift that I could not keep it from the human child.

We had fallen to sleep exhausted. All of us. By the intensity of grief over Mara's passing and the coming of the boy and the breaking of the promise; and the exquisite luxury of being human beings once again; it overtook us.

All of these things played against us. We were; in looking back; overwhelmed ourselves.

The boy could not know this. He was lost. And so were we.

He was lost in our world and we were lost in his.

Sallon sensed this. I am so overwhelmed in this moment by the seeming of this world. It feels so real. But I know this to be an illusion.

I know as the boy knows, that we are as dust; a wisp of time; and that soon; I will smile with Sallon in the great gift he made. It seems great in the moment.

But the moment passes. It is only a remembering.

It is an unfolding.

It seems real. But there is a greater reality. One that awaits us all.

We found Tesla and the boy upon the beach, wrapped slumbering together in their robes. The boy had aged. Tesla had completed his healing and spent the early morning hours teaching him. They had slept little. The boy had become a man.

He was not as I had found him adrift. He was more than I had found him. He was changed. There is no point now in concealing his identity. I Ie has the name we have given him.

His name is Davitch. He is one among us now. His seed was planted in Tesla and there is no changing it.

Sallon, on that morning; made him one of us; and by his leaving made it so.

Tesla was pregnant. After a night of frolic, it was no great surprise.

She was radiant. She conceived during the night and was carrying his child.

She knew this.

He knew this.

I cried for her in the moment I realized what great barrier we had crossed; for it was not my intent in saving him to have ever have crossed it.

It is a dream to me now.

But it is more real than you may imagine.

Dream your dreams.

They are soon to become more than a dream.

We have often played with humans. We have sent our emissaries to teach your scientists of our skills; our ways; but you have not heard us.

We have sent our teachers to touch your children; to heal them; to show you that we have a way; but you still have not heard us. We have sent our males and females to show you of our abilities; to teach you what you yourselves are capable of; but you are blind and deaf to what we teach.

You are a blind, fumbling species at times. You are so human.

In one night; Tesla taught the boy. In one crossing of the moon; the boy became a man. In one night he became as we are. His mind; like Tesla's womb; was opened to a seed.

Yes. We broke a promise.

But we made one as well.

The seed, like our promise; it grows.

You think you know who we are.

But you do not.

We seek out and find and explore depths that you have yet to see and imagine. Those depths are inside us. They are not of this world.

We abandoned those illusions many centuries ago.

They were our downfall.

Our young are born as yours are; but they are born with a different will; a different purpose than yours. Where yours are born to forget; ours are born to remember. In our whistles and our clicks our young are taught to see and hear long before human young.

They are born with a sentience that is beyond anything human beings find when they awaken here.

Our young are no where near as helpless as are the human young when they are birthed. We do not kill our young before they are born. We do not conceive of life, nor do we end it; with the same indiscretion as you.

You have no idea of the gift it is to give life to the unborn. Had you any idea of the true value of life in this world; you would not cheapen it by ending it.

You would question instead the purpose for ending life, any life; and the reasons for taking it as quickly or as easily as you do. It would not be the priceless thing you pretend it so easily and so commonly to be.

We suckle our young as do you.

But we do not poison our young at the teat as you are want to do.

Just as our species is being killed off and perishing one by one; so too is yours slowly dying.

What harms our existence; harms yours as well.

We call him Davitch. He has Sallon's mark. He wears Sallon's mark upon his wrist. He carries Sallon's mark upon the palm of his human hand. This is how you will know him.

You may doubt him. But this is how you may know him.

Sallon left his keys upon the beach and departed without so much as a farewell. He knew the boy would one day tell you of him. This is the price Sallon paid.

I hope it was worth it.

I found Sallon's keys laying upon his robe on the sunrise and I knew immediately what Sallon's old spirit had given this human child.

The golden circlets taken from Sallon's wrists meant one thing for him and quite another for the boy.

For Sallon it meant a certain untimely death in the sea. He would die as ordinary dolphins die or as an ordinary human does. Or if he chose; he himself could once again; one last time; return to land to live out his remaining years as a human and die a human death.

For me. It meant that I would never hear his thoughts again.

For me. It meant that he was lost to me until I myself had fled this life to the next.

Davitch would do well to listen to my voice as he lifted himself dreamily from his robes. There are few sacrifices in life that match a sacrifice as this.

Pay attention child; and listen well, Davitch; for in your human years; you are no where near as old as I.

I am angry; of this, let there be no doubt; at the price my beloved one has paid for your continued existence among us.

In truth; I was angry at myself. I was to blame for all of this. Davitch was only human.

Sallon was an ancient. He had descended from the Deluge.

Humans believe we live and die as they do. But they are mostly wrong about this. They are so wrong about so many things.

They believe. But belief entails faith and faith implies doubt. That means they do not know for certain.

The ones of us who have been captured have died of loneliness. We sensed that in the boy. We sensed his loneliness.

We make no secret of our human likenesses. Who would choose to live in a concrete pond, alone; separated; when the vastness of the ocean awaits?

How many humans have taken us for dumb animals?

We eat and breathe as you do.

But we love and grieve as you do as well.

What you do not know is that many of us come from a time and a place that is buried in your memories. Some of you remember us in some part. But in the others; you choose to forget us.

Davitch was angry enough to let all of you go.

He hated himself and all of you enough to love us for just one moment.

That was the gate into which we entered.

Or it was the door through which he fled.

You decide.

It matters not to me.

He carries Sallon's mark.

He has Sallon's keys.

He is one of us now whether you care to believe it or not. It; like so many other things; cannot be undone. He has mixed his blood with ours. The color of it has changed us all forever. He is more ours than yours. He cannot function in your world in any way you could say would be reliably, because he does not crave the things your young have been taught to crave. But he is indeed a child Master in ours.

Return him to us. He knows the way. Give him back to us.

He will in his last days among you; return to us. We are certain of that.

That was my only promise to him. He may return when he chooses.

I will keep that promise; even though I have broken so many others.

I cannot explain everything. I will leave that for Davitch to do.

He has a much better grasp of your limited understanding than I do.

I am lost so completely now in my grief of the reality that my world is coming to a close. The only comfort I take is of the same salt of the tears which he sheds now.

For our worlds are indeed colliding.

At the intersection of that collision there is a coming together; a joining of spirit my mother used to speak about. I take solace in this knowing that I am but a small part of the ocean in which he and I both swim.

I bent down and felt the heaviness of the keys that Sallon left behind. They were old and worn. How many centuries had he carried them?

He was an ancient. He was a guilty one. He had fled in the Deluge.

His voice had whispered to us all.

Be cautious. Life is dangerous. You have but one life. Live well.

So live it well.

His silence became a voice that resonated in the solitude of my choices. Here I was on an empty beach. I had Sallon's keys in my hand.

Keys are really locked doors. Locked doors are choices we walk through.

Doors are choices we make.

Keys are the circumstances we make those choices with. I had two circles of gold within my hand. Do I give them to Davitch and allow him to unlock a door to a world he has no idea exists?

Worse. What of Tesla and her unborn child? Her man-child?

Do I let Davitch starve on a deserted island protected from the eyes of man?

Do I trust him with these keys?

Do I seal my fate by giving them to him?

Davitch. This boy I saved and now must kill?

I should have let him drown. It would have been a small thing in comparison to the secrets I was about to share with him.

Take these.

Davitch. I will see that you will slowly starve if you laugh at these gifts. I will see that you perish a slow and agonizing death.

If you laugh and make small the greatness the gift these rings of gold represent, you will not live long enough to hear the echo of your own laughter.

Take these.

This is what I said to him.

I didn't say it.

I thought it.

Tesla translated it.

She said, "Davitch. You are named now among us. Do you object?"

He was silent. His silence was his consent. He did not object. He was truly alone in the world. His was a world of unfolding moments. He was like a wave pulled by the unseen force of the moon.

His whole demeanor was silent. Rigid. On trial. He was indeed a stranger lost in a strange world.

He sensed the magnitude of the ocean and his small place in it. He was a tiny fish in a sea of sharks, an ocean of whales. He didn't fit in our world anymore than we fit in his. We were all struggling in the confusion of it all.

Tesla continued.

"Davitch. I beg you. Be cautious in your response. Eden has the power of life and death over all that wanders in the sea. She is Keeper of our Way."

""Should you disappoint her with your answer; we will each of us disappear with the setting of this sun."

"And you will starve here alone; as though you never existed at all. And I will bear our son alone. Is this what you would choose? Or you may come with us? Please. Come with me. Leave your world behind... please..."

"Now is the moment of your choice." she pleaded.

Davitch knew.

Tesla had told him of my sister's death. He knew full well the events and circumstances that had brought him to this place.

Tesla had taught him well.

He knew the meaning of the cavern beneath him which held secrets that we would not allow him to reveal. The beach upon which he sat held secrets that would cost him more than he was willing in that moment to spend.

Tesla was asking him to come with us. She had my sanction in this.

Sallon had departed. He would never return to this place. It was impossible for him now to return. He had left the only thing that would have allowed him to return as a final silent gift for the boy. He had left his keys for Davitch.

The silent exchange was fast and certain and truthful and honest.

Sallon was gone from my world forever. The boy still remained.

Davitch stood.

I was impressed.

I am 702 years old as you have come to count them. Davitch was an infant in my eyes.

He was no longer embarrassed by his nakedness. He looked at me with the look of a man who has faced a plank or a gallows. There was no fear in his eyes and no hesitation in his thoughts.

"I will come with you."

"I have no where else to go. I have no family. I have no one else to love."

"If you will have me."

"Come then." I said. "Enough of this."

So it was then that the bracelets of Sallon were given to a human child on a hidden beach somewhere deep within the Sargasso Sea.

The longer we tarried on this beach; the more human we would become. At some point; there would be no escape. None of us knew where that point was; but it was approaching on the horizon like a summer storm. Out of no where; fast, furious, and silent.

For us; it would be as deadly as it was certain.

It was better that the boy should become as we are. The sooner we departed this place; the better. The sooner we returned to the sea; the sooner we would return to the promise we had made to keep; not break.

So it was I who broke the promise that we made in the Great Deluge nearly 12,700 years ago in your counting.

So it was I; Eden, Keeper of our Way; who has in part; invited the coming of the shift.

I did not know of it when I did it. My mother spoke of it. Perhaps she knew in that moment that I was to be a harbinger of it. She did not say.

But it comes. You can not stop it. Nor can the boy, Davitch; as we have come to call him; but he can tell you many of the things in your world that you must watch for.

We have already seen the things in ours.

I think it is too late for us.

But I do not think it is too late for you.

All in good time.

We shall see.

All in good time.

"Sit boy. I am not done with you yet. We have much to discuss."

Chapter Seven

"I am on the outside looking in. I am unspoken, whispered word."
"I will become the inmate looking out. The silent rages heard."

My mother was a waitress. Ha! She is a dead waitress. Ha! She is dead. No. She is alive. It is her shell which is dead.

"Tell me what you remember, Davitch. Take me there."

It is raining.

The cars are all green.

They are loading her coffin into the hearse. Men in black. It is raining on everybody.

I am bored. I am playing with the ashtray in the car. We are driving down the muddy road with all the stones planted here. It is the cemetery. We are in the cemetery.

I am in the cemetery. I am nine again, Eden.

A man in black opens my door. It is raining. It is raining on everybody.

Calling. Eden; I hear the calling. It is a calling. They are coming.

"Deep. Davitch. You can go deeper."

"You will come when I call. You will hear my voice above all others."

"Taste. Smell. Hear. Feel. But you are safe. You will feel it all again."

"But you will not be injured by it. You will hurt; but you will not be injured."

"Go deeper. I will be with you. This wound must be healed before you can wield the love we are about to bestow upon you."

"Go back now."

"Where did you bury the treasure?"

"Where is your treasure buried?"

Deep. How deep is this love? Eden? How deep is this love?

I buried my mother in a warm, drizzling, gentle June rain, it whispered, the rain....it whispered....in a soft patter on her glistening wooden coffin.

I cannot hear the preacher man.

All I hear is the soft patter of the rain on the lid of the casket. All I hear are the drops of water on the finished pine. The drops of rain are peeling and running; finding the smooth curve of the casket as it waits for the final drop.

The rain is dripping off the polished brass handles into the wet gaping hole of the grave beneath it.

It looks deep, Eden.

It is such a thing of beauty; the polished wood. What a shame to bury it in such a wet, dirty hole. It is deeper than any hole I have ever dug.

There is a woman I do not know holding my hand as the preacher man speaks. I don't understand what he is saying. I look up at her. I do not know her. I do not recognize her. She is weeping. She is not you, Eden.

I am wearing a suit that does not fit. It is too big for me.

I am not old enough for this suit.

I am nine.

Soon I will be ten.

My brother is standing next to me. He is seven. He looks at me and shrugs to me in the rain as if to say "What are we doing here in the rain?"

He does not understand.

She is not there. You are not here. In a moment in time far from this place he will be dead.

I have told him this because I love him. He doesn't hear me. He will kill himself because he cannot find me. It is my fault. But he is with me now.

I will not cry. She is not there. We will not cry. Men do not cry. We are men now. I smile to him and the woman jerks my hand.

She is angry with me now. She is hurting me. She is squeezing my hand hard. She is trying to hurt me. Because I am smiling at my brother.

I will remember this place. The willows mark the spot. Pirates mark their spot. Pirates mark the spot where they bury their treasure.

The preacher man hums on through the soft patter of the rain. He is humming.

The people lining the grave step forward and bend over and take a handful of wet dirt from the edge of the hole. Everyone here is a stranger to me. I do not recognize anyone. They are like ghosts.

There is a heavy "thunk" as the beautiful wooden box drops into the hole. The men in black pull the straps out and stand back from the grave. The preacher man closes his book and his mouth at the same time. He is a ghost, like in a mist..

One by one, the people standing in the rain step forward and drop their dirt into the hole. My suit, which doesn't fit me, is wet now. I have a handful of wet dirt clenched in my fist too.

I don't remember reaching for it. My fist is closed tightly around it; I am squeezing it hard like the woman squeezed my hand. I am squeezing the dirt out through my fingers. I love the feel of it. It is mud. It is warm and smells like the earth and rain...sweet.

It is wet and warm; and smells of the earth and the rain; clean; and pure. It is a mud in my fist.

"Deeper. Davitch. Go deeper. To swim with us is to go deeper."

The clumps of falling mud make eery heavy thumps against the doomed and shining wood. Solid, like bone against bone. Final. This is the end place.

My falling dirt makes a hollow clattering sound; like marbles flung across a lacquered wooden floor. She jumps. I wipe my empty hand on my pants.

The woman jerks my hand harder this time. I spooked her. I have made a mess of the dirt and the mud on my pants. It is only dirt, mud.

She's mad at me for wiping the mud on my pants. She's angry. We walk slowly to the car. Everybody is leaving now. They are in a hurry now because the rain is coming harder now. They have a lot of dirt to shovel. The green carpet is in a pile.

They are really shoveling now. It is a big pile of dirt. The pile on the left is bigger than the pile on the right. I know my right from left. My starboard from my port. A third man gets out of a truck and walks over and picks up a shovel. It is really raining now. They are really shoveling now. It is time to bury the dead.

The dirt is dry. They are shoveling dry dirt now. The rain hasn't made it there. Dry dirt. Easy to shovel. It is my mother they bury. Time to turn away.

The woman jerks my hand again. We are at the car.

It is a big hole.

So this is a grave.

So this is a graveyard. Bone yard.

I want to say goodbye. But I can't. I want to cry but I won't. My brother is watching. He is listening. He is waiting to see what I do. I am a man now. My childhood is over.

That's what is whispered in my ear.

Like a secret.

"It is time to be a man and men don't cry. Your childhood is over and it is time for you to be a man. You want to be a man, don't you?"

Yes.

I want to be a man.

"Deeper. When I call you, Davitch, you must come."

They are all drunk now. Everyone is laughing now. It is a big people laughing; big, phony belly laughs that sound scared. They echo through the house. Echoes...

"Davitch...go deeper...deeper."

Go outside and play.

The rain has slowed and stopped. It is sticky in this suit which does not fit me. The house smells of stale beer and cigarette smoke. I can hear the liquor bottles clink against the glasses.

No one is crying. They are all drunk now. Talking. Laughing. They are talking about us. They want us outside. What are we going to do with them?

She is not here.

She is not coming home.

She is never coming back.

I cannot see her, my mother.

Even in this dream, Eden, is she hidden from me.

A man takes me out on the porch. He paws me as though he loves me, but I know it is the liquor. He doesn't love me.

He's afraid of me.

All I can see is a warmth.

A billowing, cottony; opened-armed warmth.

She is taller than me. Her belly. I can feel the softness of her belly; my face against her belly. I can hear her heart beating; warm. I can feel her warmth.

The warmth of her embrace.

Stroking my hair; her warmth. The warmth of her touch. I feel safe. I feel loved. I cannot see her. I cannot see her. I cannot see her. Why can I not see her?

BACK! Back. Go back. I want to go back.

My mother is thirty-three years old. She kills herself.

I am nine. Soon I will be ten.

Next month I will be ten.

There are only two weeks left of school.

She gave me a Timex watch for my birthday. My ninth birthday. I found the watch with her graduation ring. They were going to throw them away.

Back. Go back. Please, Eden, I want to go back.

"Deeper. Davitch, breathe as we have taught you, you can go deeper."

I have the watch. I am wearing the watch. I love the watch. It takes a licking and keeps on ticking.

Everything else is stolen.

There is nothing else. Everything else is gone.

The house is gone. Dust.

It was a good house. Bad things. Good house.

I am in fourth grade. Oh..God. I love my teacher. She loves me. She is in so much pain for me. She loves me and grieves for me. It is too much for her. She leaves before the school year ends. She leaves before I can tell her goodbye. She leaves before I can tell her that I love her, too.

I love you, too. I love you, too. Please. Don't leave me here alone. Please. Don't go away too. Please.

"Deeper, Davitch....go deeper."

Her great grandfather invented a brand of barbed wire.

She knows. I think everybody knows.

Everybody I love is leaving.

I hate the substitute teacher.

I can tell by her eyes. I feel dirty when she looks at me. I feel guilty when she talks to me. It is only for a few days.

Go back. I WANT TO GO BACK!

"Go deeper."

My mother gave me a fiberglass bow and arrow set for Christmas. The arrows had suction cups on the ends that would make them stick to the walls. "Be careful you don't shoot your brother with it." my mom says.

Secrets. So many secrets. So many deep secrets. Everything is a secret. This is a secret. Don't tell anyone. This is our secret. Back...

"Deeper. There will be no secrets among us, Davitch."

It rained that summer. It rained all summer long.

I look through the streaks of rain and I cannot see her. I cannot see her. "Back...go back. Slowly".

"Deeper. Davitch. I am here. Go deeper."

I can't see anything.

All I see. All I can see is a pale corpse with a shattered, swollen face laying coldly in a polished wooden box. It is not her. It is painted to resemble her. It is like Halloween.

It is not her.

Now I smell it.

The perfume. They have doused the body with it. Roses. Attar of roses.

She is drenched with it.

I want to vomit.

All I can smell now is the sick, sweet stench of dead things. The sweet stench of too many flowers in a closed room. It is hot in here and there is this smell of death that the roses cannot cover. It is the smell of cut flowers and cold flesh decaying in the heat.

I scream until they let me go.

I will not kiss it goodbye. I will not touch it's hand.

It is not my mother.

My mother is alive and warm and she loves me and she would not leave me here alone.

"Deeper, Davitch. Go beyond this place."

Who will love me now? If she is gone; who will love me now!?

It is not her. It cannot be her. Please. Oh, please. Who will love me, us; who will love me now? Eden...please...no more...bring me back....no more...oh please....

No. Eden. I can go no deeper. There is nothing there. It is darkness. Nothing. There is nothing left there. Darkness.

"Davitch. There is. Go deeper."

I killed her! It's my fault! I killed my brother! I'm so sorry.... Forgive me.... I should have let him sleep. It is all my fault.... There is nothing left to love. It is all gone. Everything. Everybody....they are all gone. I am alone...I deserve this....

Oh..God...kill me.... Kill me too! Please kill me too. Please! Who will love me now? Will anyone ever love me now?

"Davitch; we will love you. The dream. Tell me of your dream?"

"Deeper. I am your light in this darkness. Go deeper."

It was a lie, Eden. Please...it was no dream...it was a nightmare.....

"No. It was a truth."

It was a lie.

"It is a truth. How is it that you knew before they came to wake you?"

I heard them coming. Please, Eden. I cannot swim this deep...go...

"No. You knew before they came. You could always tell before. It is a gift. It is not a curse."

"Go deeper. I promise I will not abandon you. You are safe in the love of another. It is time. There can be no secrets among us. What did she say to you?"

It was a lie. I am lying. I am lying. Please. I made a mistake. Please. No. Please. I will do anything.

"Then go deeper."

A stand of willows. Weeping willows. I am naked. There is a stairwell. I am standing naked in a grove of weeping willows. There is a stairwell that reaches down through the branches of the willows. The branches gently reach to touch me as I come to the foot of the stairwell.

"Deeper. Go deeper...."

My mother is there. She is waiting there.

"What is she doing there?"

She is waiting for me.

"She has something to say to you. I want you to tell me what she says."

I cannot. I am so ashamed of who I am. I am so ashamed of what has happened to me. Please let me die, Eden,...please.... Please. I cannot bear this.

"Davitch. Listen to me. What do you see?"

I see my mother standing on the stairwell.

"What is she saying to you?"

KILL ME! Please. Let me die...

"No. Tell me what she is saying to you."

Forgive me. She is saying forgive me. She is saying "Davitch...please... Forgive me."

"Yes. So look at her."

I cannot. I want to go with her. But she will not take me. I am so ashamed and I know she is leaving and I want to go with her. I don't want her to leave me here. I will do anything. Please. Don't leave me here alone.

I love you...please...don't leave me here alone.

"What else is she saying?"

She loves me. She loves me more than I know. She loves me more than I love her...more than I love her...more than I love her.

"Davitch. I love you more than you love me. I am so sorry. Please forgive me. It is not your fault. Keep my love for you alive."

I will. I promise. They're coming. Take me with you. Please. Mom. Please. Please......please.

Oh, God. Kill me now. I beg you.

"You know you cannot come with me you silly boy! You have a wonderful life to live and many wonderful gifts to give."

"Davitch. Look at her. Look at your mother."

I can't. She won't love me if she sees me like this.

"She will always love you. You are her son. Listen. What do you hear?"

I hear your voice, Eden...Please let me drown....let me go.....

"No, Davitch. What else do you hear?"

I hear a summertime song. It is one of those that play when its hot songs. Downtown. Things will be fine when were downtown. I can hear

94

a whistle, your whistle, and a siren. No. I hear a siren in the distance. It is a siren wailing.

"Now. Go deeper, Davitch."

I hear banging on a door. Someone is banging on a door somewhere. I cannot see. It is dark. All I hear is banging. I can smell strawberries. It is the strawberry patch from across the road.

It is summertime. It is hot. It is nighttime. I hear a radio playing. Someone is banging on a door.

We call it the dog patch. He calls me his "Lil Abner."

I can smell the strawberries from the patch across the road. There is a farm across the road. I am two? No. I am three. My brother is not here yet.

Soon. He will be here soon.

I hear my father calling. He is angry. He has her.

No. Eden. No.

"Come here, you miserable bitch!" "You fucking miserable, ungrateful bitch!"

It sounds like clapping. But it isn't. I can make the sound. Two hands coming together fast and hard. Flesh meeting flesh. It sounds white. Pounding white.

Heavy. Heaving. Groaning. Whimpering. A sigh.

"You called the fucking cops you miserable! fucking! CUNT!"

"I'll! Teach! You! You! You! Fucking! Whore!"

Crashing.

Silence. I hear.

I hear your clicks, Eden. I hear your whistle.

Silence growing in the sound of clapping.

Colors. Many flashing colors running by.

Blue. Red. Silver.

"Slut!" And then silence. There is nothing but silence.

"Look around you, little one. Where are you?"

I am in a field of strawberries. I am laughing. It is a joy here. It is sun and warm and green everywhere. I am alive. I am in the world. Everything is sweet. I can hear my mother's laughter. We are eating strawberries.

The farmer's bull is coming.

I see him.

My mother does not.

The farmer has let his bull out to roam. The farmer does not know we are here. The bull can hear us. He doesn't know where we are. He can't see us. He is looking for us.

The bull is coming.

I am...there is nothing beyond this place. Go back now. It is deep here. There is nothing beyond here but dreams.

The bull is coming. It is bad here.

No deeper. The bull sees her.

"No. Davitch. The bull does not see her. It sees you."

"Go deeper."

She is running now. The men have crossed the road. They have seen the bull. They are waving and yelling at the bull. They are throwing bottles at the bull and running toward it. One of them has pulled his belt off. He is waving it in the air.

I am laughing.

My mother is running away. She has kicked off her shoes. I can see her long blond hair flowing in the wind as she runs away from me. She looks like Neva. The bull is chasing her. It will not catch her. She runs with a laugh in her heart.

The men turn the bull and chase it away.

She is coming for me. She is laughing and crying and smiling. I love her. She is strawberries. Strawberry. Sweetness. I am. I love her.

I must go back now the way I came, Eden. It is too deep here.

"No. You must go deeper still."

There is nothing but dreams there.

"That is where you are wrong, Davitch."

"Go deeper. Listen to my clicks; listen for my whistle."

It is warm here. I am loved here. There is Love here. She is here somewhere, around me. I can stay. I can feel her here. It is only love here.

No. I can go no further.

"No. You must go deeper."

"What do you hear?"

I hear a car engine racing. It is angry. It is growling. There is a hurt there. There is hurt there. Salt? Salty? It is wet salt? Am I bleeding?

"No, Davitch. You are weeping. Go deeper."

"Where are you?"

I am in darkness. Darkness. I am surrounded by darkness. I am in a bed that does not fit me. It is growling below my window. There are angry voices mixed with the growling engine.

Now the voices are screaming. One voice

"Cunt! I'm gonna kill every fucking one of ya's!"

He is out there. My father. Soon he will be dead.

My mother. She is dead.

He has found us. They are dead.

More voices. Hush. Hush hush. Hush hush hush. He is gone angry.

He is gone angry and drunk.

Fear?

So this is hate?

"Yes Davitch. This is hate. This is how humans learn. Go deeper."

"Find her in the darkness."

I cannot.

"Where are you?"

It is morning. It is early morning. We are on a road. It is hot in the morning. It was cool in the darkness but now it is hot. I am tired.

We are on a road. It is a long road. All I can see are her eyes in the mirror. They are blue. They are a sparkling blue, like my brother's. They are like your's Eden. She is telling me in her eyes that she loves me. I can see her smile in her eyes. They are like Shayne's, blue, like the ocean.

I cannot hear her.

We are alone on the road.

Her hair is gold. Blond. Like Ebron's. Long. Like Neva's. And it smells like white ivory soap.

I love her. I love her scent. It is clean; like wet earth during a rain....

"What else do you see?"

A brown building. Filled with negroes. Black people. We are white. We are in a ghetto.

It is where her brother lives.

She has fled here. She is a refugee.

The building is tall. It is a ghetto. Everybody here is black except her brother. He is like a black sheep. He is a black sheep. But he fits here.

He is judged. Like them.

My brother is here with us. He is arrived.

He arrived before we did. He was born on the way.

He is three. I am five. My father cannot find us here. He does not know of this place. We are hidden here. We are hiding in plain sight.

"Tell me what happened to you here?"

I am killed here.

I was an accidental departure.

"So how is it that you are here today?"

I don't know.

"But you do."

No.

"Yes. You do."

She is running now. My mom. I am laying in the road. She is barefoot. She is barefoot, and holding me. Like the day with the bull. On the stairwell. She is barefoot. Like you, Eden. She is barefoot.

The paperboy has told her. I am laying in the road. There is blood in my nose. In my mouth. In the corners of my eyes. I have been hit by his car.

I see her running. She is running like the wind. I am above her.

I am behind her.

She is in the road with me and the man has stopped his car and he is just standing there crying. He is trying to talk to her. She is kneeling in the road.

I am cradled in her arms. People are coming. I am not moving.

I hear the siren now.

I hear the sirens now.

He is saying, "I didn't see him, lady. Honest to Christ. He was just there. He just stopped dead in his tracks. I swear, lady, I never even saw him."

I hear my mother now.

She is saying; "Oh my God... Davitch...Davitch...Davitch..don't die. Oh sweet Jesus; don't take my little boy; please; don't take my little boy."

I am warm all over, Eden. But she is not here. It is a fuzzy warm light. She is the other way. But I can still hear her.

"What do you hear, Davitch?"

A calling, Eden. I hear a calling. She is calling to me. The warm light is calling, too. She is calling me. "Davitch! Don't you dare! Don't you dare leave me like this. Do you hear me!"

I love her. But I love the warm light, too. "You can stay if you want." But I love her, yes. "Yes, you do." "You will always love her. And she will always love you; but you may stay if you choose."

A time passed. It seemed like a moment to me. A day? No. Many days. And I know she loved me because she came to get me. She came to find me in that place. She came to get me from that place. I was awake. It was a hospital.

She came to take me home.

"Where are you now, boy?"

I am not sure. We took the long road after that. A great deal of time passed.

Some time has passed. I'm not sure. We are on the long road and it ends in the letters of the alphabet.

I am in the car. It is a white station wagon. I am at the A&P. I have a book in my hand. Dick & Jane. It is just a book with pictures. It was about Dick and Jane. I can't remember the name of the book. All I remember is that I was in the parking lot of the A&P.

When will this interrogation end, Eden?

"When you are ready to wear Sallon's gold."

"What happened in that place?"

A&P. A&P. This is the A&P. See Dick run. See Jane. See Spot. Run Dick. See See See at the A& Pee Pee Pee..I can read...my God...I can read. My God!

I can read! Eden...

"Do you see now, young one?"

In the parking lot of the A&P pee... pee...

Mom! Mom! Mom! I can Read! I CAN READ!

"No child. You can do more than read now. The question is; what shall you do with that ability?"

Oh..mom...I love you so much. Eden...I can read. Go back. Go back.

"No. Davitch. Go Deeper."

Ma. It hurts. My arm has been broken. He is here. His arm is broken too.

He is touching me now.

"Deeper."

Yes. It is time. He is touching me now. I am not safe anymore. My mother does not know this. He will kill me in the dark.

"It is too deep here, Eden. Eden I will Drown Here!!!!!Go back!"

I will panic and drown here! Where is your whistle? Where is your click?

Do not abandon me here! He will kill me in the dark! I have to tell my mother! He will kill me! He is killing me! Over and over again!

"Come to me now, child. Boy, come to my voice. You are safe here."

It is raining now?

"No, Davitch. It is not raining. You have been weeping. You are safe. It has been too long. Men do cry. Especially nine year old boys."

"You are a man now. Your boyhood is over."

"You will come with us, Davitch."

"If you will have us."

"If you will love us."

Chapter Eight

I could read Tesla's thoughts. She was offering them gently to me. They were like a plate of tender fruit; spread out in humble grace; beautiful and splendid in their sweet innocence.

She was holding Sallon's bracelets in her hands. I had given them to her. Davitch was cradled in her arms. I had taken him deeper than he had ever been before. He was in shock. He would recover shortly.

He would go deeper. He was strong. Stronger than I had first believed.

It was a surprise to me that he had survived at all. Few humans would have survived the ordeal he had been through as a child. It was better that he should learn our ways upon the safety of the beach.

The waters of the open sea had their own measure of perils.

Tesla would be his mentor; his playmate. Her thoughts in the moment were a sweet solace to the boy.

You should taste of them before you depart. She will speak soon.

Perhaps you will linger yet a bit longer and listen as this story winds its way forward.

It is a difficulty among our species. We learn to guard against it. There is nothing to hide. We are not like humans. We do not live in ambiguity. There is no duplicity.

We are a complex, yet simple creature.

We do not know how to lie.

Humans on the other hand; are a complex creature as well; yet filled with and constructed of all manner of deceptions. All humans beings know are deceptions and half-truths.

From the moments of your births you are taught lies, and competitions, and differences. You are not taught what you have in common; but only what you have in differences.

You are not taught to see your similarities.

You are only taught to see what each of you have in values.

This will change very soon.

What unites you as a species will very soon divide you.

This may very well mark your end as a race and spell your downfall. You cannot see it because you are standing in the middle of it. But we can see it.

We are on the outside looking in.

We could not see it for ourselves. It was a difficult lesson for our species to learn.

The boy can see it. He is on the outside looking in.

You would do well to listen to him.

We have seen it before. Many thousands of years ago.

Our species are proof of it.

We were human once ourselves.

This planet is alive in a way we did not understand. The universe is alive in a way we did not understand.

You are only now beginning to grasp the truth and the magnitude of this.

For us; the understanding of this came too late.

We did not know this when we started our journey here. No one who comes here does. Not even you. It takes many lives here to understand that all life here is connected; that all life here is interdependent; that all life here is one.

We were pioneers on a virgin frontier. We came to this planet with a single purpose in mind.

Our purpose; when we discovered this planet; was to incarnate in the realm of the absolute physical nature and beauty of this world, and seek and find a balance in it.

We failed miserably.

There were only a few of us who returned at first. We colonized the earth and mixed with the blood of the seeds of the offspring we had planted here. Our technology far surpassed anything the pioneers we had left behind had developed up to the point of our return.

Your religions and history books speak of us. But they do little to explain who we are or why we came. They do not explain what happened to us or how we came to disappear completely in just one day from the face of the earth.

Davitch knows.

Our first journey in the ocean with him was to the place of Sallon's birth. We took him to the old places; to the Appa Sea.

It was there that we showed him the submerged ruins of our first coming.

But I leap ahead of myself.

Tesla slowly brought Davitch back. He was silent. He was amazed at the opening of his mind. It is another gift we have made to him. It is one that also cannot be undone.

She had slipped Sallon's bracelets upon his wrists.

The bracelets allowed Davitch immediate access to my thoughts if I chose. They allowed him immediate access to many other things if he chose.

I watched as the bracelets slowly melted to conform to the contours of his wrists. He was visibly fascinated as he felt the cool metal melt around them. He looked up at me in question.

"They are a gift. They are a great gift. Wear them well. Use them wisely. They will allow you to go places your kind can only dream of going."

"Sallon has paid a great price for you to see the things you are about to see. He has sacrificed more than you can imagine for you to learn the things you are about to learn. So pay attention. Learn well the lessons I am about to teach you boy."

It was time for us to leave.

Tesla and Davitch rose. Ebron and Neva had watched silently from a few yards away as I took Davitch into the depths of my mind.

It was time to return the robes and close the sanctuary.

We walked back through the palms into the clearing.

I watched as Davitch traced his hand along the pearl encrusted walls of the stairwell leading down into the hall. Ebron took the robes and sandals from us and disappeared into one of the anterooms.

I took one last look around.

I could not know when I would; if I ever would; return to this place.

We climbed the stairwell silently and stood naked in the warm sunlight.

Tesla held the hand of the boy as Neva stepped forward and touched her wrist to the circle of gold on the portal.

It rumbled shut.

She raised her hands above her head, closed her eyes; and touched her wrists together. The dais began a slow descent into the clearing from which it had risen.

Davitch watched wide-eyed as the huge stone vault disappeared into the ground. There was barely any trace of the earth ever having been disturbed.

We turned in unison and walked quietly back to the beach.

I had come to this place to say farewell to my sister Mara. Instead, I have said farewell to her and my beloved Sallon as well.

Now we have a human child as companion.

What crime against nature have I committed?

Is it a crime to take him with us?

It did not feel like one.

The next few moments would say for certain; for we were leaving.

I looked at Davitch. Sallon's gold had indeed melted into his wrists. It was as though they were meant for him. He wore them without any vanity or thought to them at all.

They were like a long forgotten bruise to him.

He was indeed a male.

We will see how well he will do in the sea. Let us see how well he fares in the face of teeth sharper than his own.

We entered the water together.

The change was predictable.

Davitch choked and rolled to the surface. It was not unexpected. He was; how should I put it; like a fish out of water?

No. He was overwhelmed.

The transformation was immediate and complete.

He no longer had a human voice.

He no longer had human legs or hands.

He was in many ways a fish.

But we are not as fish. We feed upon fish.

We are mammals. We are as you are.

His thoughts were in a panic. His whistles and clicks came in rapid and frightened pulses. He was like a young one first birthed from the warmth of the womb.

They were a joy to us in the moment. Tesla was there beside him. He was like a foundling. Thrashing. Struggling to find his balance, his equilibrium.

He was like one in the moment birthed from the womb. He was a pup.

"Now do you understand?"

"Davitch?"

"Can you hear me?"

"Davitch?"

"I can't breathe."

"Yes. You can. Find your center. The gold is the center. Find it."

"Yes. I see it. I can breathe now."

It was Tesla speaking to him. I was just watching. I was just snickering.

He could hear me snickering. Click click click. Snicker snicker snicker. It was a playful snicker.

"I can't breathe."

"No. What frightens you the most now, Davitch; is that you have no opposable thumbs. What panic you feel is that your legs are gone. In their place is something you haven't even begun to discover yet."

I watched as Tesla rolled beside him.

"Watch me." she said.

Tesla bent her body and shot straight up into the air; clearing the surface; using only her powerful tail fin to propel her upward. She came splashing downward within inches of Davitch.

He just laid there on the surface like some paralyzed, stunned grouper waiting to be netted.

"I'm afraid to move."

"No. You are just afraid."

"Fear is the price that your choice to join us has cost you. So move. The absolute worst that will happen to you is that you will drown. You have already faced that fear. So move."

"Discover the gift that Sallon has made to you."

He did. He began to move. Slowly at first. But he moved.

Tesla is a wonderful teacher.

He quickly became a very adept student. I have said it before. He is very observant. He learns quickly. It took him less than the remainder of the morning to learn enough to travel with us beyond the reach of the lagoon.

But enough of that morning.

We returned to the sea.

We took the man-child with us.

We could not leave him there to die.

What remains of our presence on that beach are nothing more than footprints in the sand.

What remains of our presence in your world are only mysteries to man.

The great monuments to our technologies still befuddle your scientists and confuse your philosophers.

Because you cannot explain them; you dismiss our existence with a wave of your hand.

When we fled our demise; we did so with a promise on our lips.

You will likely do the same.

Every species throughout the universe makes empty promises to its creation as it dies; and does so in one last vain hope to endure.

It was our vanity that was our undoing.

It is your vanity that speaks to you now.

Do not listen to your own arrogance.

Listen instead to the boy.

Our arrogance was our undoing.

You would do well to learn from it.

Chapter Nine

"I am the blamed. The useless. The un-believed. I am the broken."
"I will become the blamed. I will be your hopeless, lying token."

I have a great task before me. I must try somehow to communicate with you the things that are beyond words. Many questions have been asked of me. I am saddened by many of them.

Love is indeed deep and pure. There is no bottom to the well from which it springs..

I really don't know where to begin. I will say this. I have worked my way through the murky waters of my grief for my mother; though it was well beyond the time for me to have been done with it. I love her still. More than any of you can know.

I know now the color of her eyes.

I know now the origin of several other things that have eluded me. I have Eden to thank for this. Things that I had long since buried with my mother are alive to me now.

I now stand much closer to the end of my journey; though I have in truth; just begun it.

I have yet to honestly assess many of the feelings that remain for her. But I know that I must and that one day soon I will. It will happen before I flee this place. Or it will happen in the moment I flee this place. I have watered the flowers upon her grave for too long now as it is.

She is not there.

She waits for me in another place.

It will happen. The shift is coming.

But I must say this; I have drawn closer to the end even though you cannot yet see it; even though it is yet beyond you. I am always upon the horizon.

Come with me.

We are all orphaned together.

You and I.

I did not choose Eden. She chose me. I am chosen. Many are called.

No.

All are called. Few choose. This is what she said to me.

"All are called. Few choose."

I allow the faith that I hold and the love that I feel to guide me in these days. This is the truth.

I have waited patiently for her voice to return. I knew one day that it would. It was her promise to me.

I hear the calling once again.

It is not a madness.

It is a healing.

One I have prayed for in faith and in love for a very long time to return.

I hear her whistle.

It is not my purpose I serve.

The child; that child, when he entered the water; did not grow in time as others do.

His mind did not age as others age. Time stopped within those circles of gold.

They were like a watch that would not wind and did not tick.

He is who I am. He is not what was made of him by small-willed human beings; people driven to madness by their greed or their lust.

In your compassion for him; you cannot steal his pain and the things he learned in it. It is in that pain that he has become fully human. It is in that pain that he has become fully alive.

I can love you for wanting to take it; but there is a greater gift to be had if you have the courage to endure it.

What you feel for me is but a fraction of what I felt once for myself.

It is not a self-pity.

It is a joy.

I am alive and I am free of that pain and guilt.

I am.

It is a hope that calls to me; whispers to me; and soon I will emerge from it. Soon I will be completely free of it; done with it; and stronger because of it.

Ask yourself.

Will a person's faith or love grow in the light of truth? Or will it wither away in darkness? Which will make it grow stronger? What fire will purify a soul? The cold one that barely warms your hands; or the one that blinds your eyes?

Have you forgotten everything?

I have come here to remind you.

No. I have come to remind only one of you. I need only one of you to remember.

We are only as sick as our secrets would keep us. There will be no secrets among us. There will be nothing to forgive, because you have committed no crime for which heaven will deny you. There will be no guilt to be given; there will be no blame to be had. There will be none lesser among us for a mistake that matters not.

I know many things that you do not. I will share all those things with you. I know that if you can love me in the things I will share with you; I will be free. If I purchase my freedom by doing so; I will also purchase yours. We are linked together by the same heritage.

I can promise you that there will be no celebration until all of us are safely returned home. Then will the celebration begin.

Confession is an ancient discipline.

It's benefits are well documented.

I tell you this.

I am not alone in this.

I have asked the counsel of those wiser than I; and they all agree.

So I will continue.

But I will not love anyone any less should they decide now to depart the road upon which we have embarked.

It is not for the timid or the weak of heart.

There is a great shining that will light the way. It may well be the brilliance of your pain that leads us on our road. It might well be the radiant and resplendent shining of your own shame that leads us on our way.

But there is a great benefit to be had. One that you may not understand yet.

One you may as yet reject. But in the end; you will see.

To know one's self; is to see both the beauty and the beast.

Intelligence to me has always been the ability to "find a way forward or through by skillful means." In the simplest of terms and by the simplest of measures; it is exactly what it means.

It means to find a way through and emerge on the other side.

It is to die in a way.

It is to awaken after a kind of death.

It is to awaken after the death of everything you know or believe was real has died. And to go on afterwards with a new perspective.

Eden taught me this.

One does not grow stronger by; or wiser by; avoiding the things which cause us pain.

One grows stronger by facing them; and indeed; one grows stronger by looking them in the face and calling them for what they really are.

One grows by calling them by name; and in love; refusing those things we know in our hearts to be wrong and embracing those things we know to be true.

As I stepped into the water.... I stepped into a light.

I have chosen in my heart to serve this light; which I know now to be the source of all that I know to be all that is good and true.

I could have refused. That was my one great choice in this life.

I could very well have chosen to serve the darkness.

I could have chosen to serve the fear and loneliness I know to exist within it. That is one hell.

That was given me to choose. Who would have judged me had I chose it?

Them?

I was invited. So to are you invited.

I was a guest. You are my guest.

Who would have judged me had I chosen the darkness for the evils perpetrated against me?

Great evil begets great evil.

Great love begets an even greater love.

I am proof of this.

My life is proof of this.

I know a great love. I searched a great depth in the warmth and light of it.

There is nothing I would not endure now for it.

I offer you a question. Tell me why? Why? Why of all people; having experienced the pain and depravation I have known; do I choose to serve that which seems to have been so conspicuously absent in my life?

Why?

Because I know love for what it truly is.

It is the eternal fountain from which we spring.

It is the endless spring from which we flow.

It is our source.

It is our Origin.

Tell me why we need so much the love from our children; so much do we need love from those we come to love in our short lives? If you can answer this you are indeed halfway home. For just as we need love from those who come through us and to us; so too does our Source need our love to return in some small way to it.

So too; does our Origin need our love to flow back to it in return; much like an endless river returning in kind to the endless ocean which gave it life.

Our love cannot go forever away from it.

It must one day return to the Source from which it flows.

Do not let your disbelief in this blind you in the moment.

You have nothing and everything I want. I cannot go home without you.

It is both your purpose and mine that I serve. I would see you reach home before I do. Because I cannot get there without you anymore than you can get there without me..

I have everything to gain by sharing this with you; and everything to lose by keeping it from you.

I am no longer ashamed of who I am. It is all a lie to keep us forever in chains. These lives we build around ourselves are just memories we hold for a moment and then they turn to dust and are forgotten. We believe in them. But they are not who we are. We are greater than the lies we tell ourselves. We are greater than the lies we believe others tell us about ourselves.

There was a time I was ashamed to be a human being.

I was a child once and I was ashamed of being alive. What does that say of the evils in this world? What does that say?

The silence in that question begs more questions than any of the answers I could offer or any of my words could begin to speak about it.

A human child cannot fall as far as I; nor can a human child endure as much as I; without deserving some purpose to his pain. If there is no purpose to it; then we die and it is nothing but cold and empty darkness beyond this life. Our lives blink out like a falling star and our consciousness is extinguished along with all our hopes and all our fears.

I did not perish in the mad journey. Many have. I have emerged on the other side of it with a fine gold in my hands.

I would give it to you. But you must first see it for what it is. It is unlike the gold of this world. It is made of a finer stuff.

So it is time now that I face the things that call my life from me. You may have and keep the gold. You must.

It is not of this world.

It matters to me. It will matter to you. It is the stuff of which we are made. The things of this world do not matter in the next.

My future is the same as yours. We share it. I am only one. I am as you are. My sight is the same as yours. In this world it does what yours does. It always looks back. It lies always looking back in the past. It is never looking ahead. My past is just like yours. My past is identical to yours. My past is who I think I am. I cannot let it go. I must hold it and claim it as mine.

But I will love it all into submission. And then I will forgive it away.

I loved my mother. I do not wonder in it now. I know now the depths of her despair.

She did not desert me.

Look what I found. Look what you will find. You have not been deserted by love. You have not been abandoned by your source. Your Origin has not left you orphaned in an insane hell. It loves you far too much for that.

It was not her loneliness which killed her.

It was her despair. She was not alone. She was not abandoned.

It was her pain. She believed she was alone in it.

I will not perish in mine. You will not perish in yours.

If you can for one moment love without a reason. You will be free of yours. You need only the courage to go as deep as your love will take you.

Many things come out of that grief. If you can hold that grief for one moment and understand that grief is fear, you will be free of it.

Our innocence is not taken from us. It is not stolen from us. It is not ripped from our hands in some ugly, tragic happening that changes us forever.

Mine wasn't. I abandoned my innocence. I watched my innocence as they were shoveling dirt into an empty hole. It was there. In the rain. I abandoned my innocence to an empty hole filled with an empty shell.

We abandon our innocence like a wet, shivering puppy beside an open, empty grave.

We might as well leap into that hole and cover ourselves with dirt.

We need to go back and reclaim it. No matter what it costs.

We need to go back, find it, and get it back. It belongs to us. It is our path home.

We may need to fight for it.

It is a fight that is worth fighting.

It is a fight that is worth losing over and over again. Because sooner or later we will win that fight.

Because it is worth all the fight it takes to get it back.

We cannot let our innocence die beside an empty hole that holds nothing but a hopeless darkness and the lie that death is the end. It is not the end.

Yes. I'll say it because it needs to be said. The world starves in its emotional and spiritual poverty. And nothing can fill the void.

Just as I starved in my youth; just as I starved in my loneliness, so does the world starve now believing that ignoring the grave it has dug for itself will somehow make that grave disappear.

But you must believe me when I say that you are closer to a truth than you know.

I was raised on a daily diet of hate. Hate is fear. It is the fear of being alone. It is the fear of being different. It is the fear of being unloved. It is the fear of being abandoned. It is the fear of being orphaned. Hate is fear.

Yet I love as few in this world love.

Explain that to me.

I have no education.

Yet I have the intelligence of an infant whistled in his mother's embrace.

Explain that to me.

I know many of the things I would share with you are difficult to explain and even more difficult to understand. But you will remember them. To remember means to know again.

Many of you will wonder why I have chosen you and the purpose you play in this. It simply is what it is. You may come if you so desire. Or ignore me if you choose.

Many of the things I know and feel are beyond expression; even though I have prayed for a means to share them with you.

It often seems that my life has been one obstacle after another. One hoop to jump through after another. Is your life any different?

Would you have it any other way?

It seems too; that the darkness has sought to crush in my every step the love that I hold; to turn me from my path; but it cannot.

There is nothing I value more in life than the love that I hold.

In this gift; there is nothing that can be taken from me. There is no prison cell that can imprison it. No threat that can threaten it.

But in the world of men; there are things I hold that would be hunted much like a rabid dog is hunted. The only way to silence it is to kill it. But even then the silence has a voice. Even then the silence speaks. Even then the silence sings.

What I would share will spread one thread on the wind at a time..

But it will not be welcomed in this world because this world lives on hate.

My own wounds have been opened to cleanse them so they may heal. They have festered long enough. I can no longer call them anything other than what they are. You must do the same.

It is not as hard as you may fear it to be.

I have been gentle to my own harm. It has only prolonged my

going home. I have guarded my own injuries like some bitter badge of courage.

It is time for them to heal. It is time for us to go home.

It is time.

The shift is upon us.

I could have chosen so many other ways to say this.

I have not deceived you.

I need only travel this road once more. I am weary of this place and its illusions.

Were I to decline; I would be doomed to travel it a thousand times again.

But I would be free.

I laugh at some of the things I have found for I know now what they are. Yes. Some of it was painful. Some of it hurts. But it means that I am alive. I hurt as I have never hurt before.

But the pain has fled in the light of Eden's love. I watched it run; squalling and yelping; and in the place where my pain held reign; there is now peace. The Author of that Peace will be the Author of yours. He is not the Author of confusion. He is the Author of Peace.

Do you not see yet what I do? Perhaps not. But you will find your way.

In almost every road I was given; there was choice. In almost every road I took; each conscious step I made; was there my human will rising to command.

I subdue it now to my love and my faith.

I will suffer even more pain as a cause of it in this journey; but I need only one of you to follow in your own path. Just one of you. One will be enough.

I do not ask any of you to drink a cup of grape flavored rat poison. I ask you instead to sit by my fire for one moment of your life. I do not need a thousand. I only ask for one.

I will be free of it in the end.

All of it.

I will be free. And so too will one of you.

I feel my pain, but that will pass. I would be free. I feel yours as well. That too shall pass.

I see a new hope arise in the ashes of my shame. I would that you would be free of yours as well. You may give all your guilt to me. I am as guilty as any of you.

There is a child lost within us all. Find yours as I have found mine.

Whatever you would ask of me; I would without any question give or share with you.

It is a rare thing to take such a risk. But I have learned that the only risks in life we live to regret are the ones we do not take.

I recognize now how easily our lives pivot on a single step. How many times in life have I stumbled in those steps?

Take one with me now. Close your eyes. Smell the salt in the air. Listen to my voice. I will take you there. Can you taste the salt in the air? Can you feel the ship pitch and yaw in the waves?

The ship is heaving in the ocean. The waves have a mind of their own. There is no pattern to them. There is no design. They are like snowflakes. They are like us. Each is different. Each comes for but a moment and is gone.

Each wave is unique in the universe. There are no two alike....

The walk aft on the ship was always the long one. It was the walk where I always took my time to watch the waves....

I could see my life gently rise and fall in the waves rolling by the sides of the ship. We were making way in a three foot swell. It was just enough to rock the boat.

It is like the motion of a cradle with a baby inside it. Slowly. Back and forth. Back and forth. It is the motion of a big, old lumbering cow slowly walking across an empty, deserted field.

I climbed down the forecastle deck and jumped the last two steps on the ladder to the main deck. The sun was shimmering off the rusted, blackened surface of the steel.

A wire cable ran the length of the sides of the vessel and served as a safety rail. It was swaying gently back and forth in the roll. Walking was a dance. It was a dance until you got used to the rhythm of the movement. The decks were empty of crew.

I always felt small moving across them. It was a little more than 200 yards. Two football fields. I could have rode a bicycle across the deck. It was a good walk. The dolphins always followed me.

They would flip and jump.

"Hey. Over here! Look at me! Bet you can't do this!"

I'd smile and wave. I only wished I could do what they could do.

On that day the air had become cooler and tasted slightly of salt. A fine mist permeated the mid-day shine and everything was coated with a salty dew. It was almost one in the afternoon. I was surprised.

It hadn't seemed like I had been an hour on the foredeck playing with the dolphins. We had just left port earlier that morning.

I had brought a loaf of stale bread with me that I had gotten from Miguel, the Mexican mess boy during lunch. The boxes of bread we had loaded that morning in the galley had been packed days in advance and the bread was already going bad. I had raced back up to the bow to watch the coastline disappear.

The dolphins had loved it.

I made my way to the aft castle and climbed the ladder that led up to the entrance to the galley.

Everything vibrated.

There was a deep, heavy, thrumming coming from the engines that gave a vibrating motion to everything that I touched.

The ship's engines were huge. A man could crawl inside the cylinders of them and probably get lost inside them if he tried. The whole stern of the ship seemed to be one gigantic engine that the rest of the ship just happened to be absently attached to.

The solitary stack that carried the company emblem was spewing an ugly black trail of diesel dust that followed the ship for several hundred yards. The trail of dust was eaten up by the light breeze that blew over the ship heading into the coast of Florida.

The crew mess hall was empty. Miguel came to the half-door that separated the galley from the crew hall and asked with a motion of his hand, "You want something to eat? Drink?"

I shook my head. "No. Where is everybody?"

He pointed outside and around the hatch that led into the interior of the crew quarters.

Ok. I gotcha.

Like it took a rocket scientist to figure out they weren't all crowded around me here in the crew mess.

Outside. Good. Ok. They didn't go bowling.

I stepped outside the hatch and listened for voices above the dull roar of the engines. Nothing.

I didn't want to be late for my watch so I set out to look for the Bosun's mate.

I walked through a couple of watertight doors to the passageway that led to the crew's quarters and found everybody standing outside a cabin that had been locked previously.

Everybody I had met on the ship was here. Andre saw me coming down the passageway. He walked up to greet me.

"So you finally decided to join us, eh?"

"What's going on?" I asked.

A man pushed by us in the passageway. We squeezed up against the bulkhead to let him pass.

The passageway was narrow and hot and filled with about fifteen men all vying for a position near the door of the cabin. They were all laughing and joking. I could barely hear Andre above the noise of their voices and the incessant thrum of the engines.

I asked again; only this time I shouted so Andre could hear me.

"What's going on?"

Andre leaned into me as the ship caught an especially large swell throwing everybody against the starboard bulkhead.. He had to shout to make himself heard above the commotion.

"We are outside the territorial limit."

"What's that mean?"

Andre grinned.

"It means that Hanz can open the ship's store. Do you want some cigarettes? Or some vodka, maybe?"

The ship's store was just that. It was a little store that had all kinds of commodities which are normally taxed inside the United States. Basically all it had was smokes and booze; but everything in the store was meant for consumption outside the United States.

Legally; the Captain of a ship couldn't open the store until he was outside the territorial limits of U.S. waters.

"I don't have any money!" I shouted. Actually; I had the twenty dollar bill in my sneaker that the Customs Officer had given me; but that was money in the bank. I wasn't touching that.

I thought it would be nice to have a bottle of vodka. If anyone deserved to get smashed, it was me.

"You don't need any!" Andre shouted back raising his eyebrows. As if to say... "How do you like them apples?"

He grabbed me by the shoulder and pushed me into the line ahead of him. He leaned over my shoulder and continued to explain.

"We passed the twelve mile limit about fifteen minutes ago.

"Hanz opened the store just after we left the Cut."

"He's been torturing the men ever since. He will start soon. He will write down whatever you take from the store and deduct it from your pay at the end of the month."

"You can draw money if you like but there is no place to spend it; unless you play dominoes. Hanz will only open the store once or twice while we are at sea so if want some vodka or cigarettes maybe you should get them now."

"You can only draw one bottle and two cartons of cigarettes at a time so I suggest you take something now."

Another man moved to make his way by and Andre shifted to let him through. He was carrying two cartons of cigarettes and a quart of Smirnoff Vodka.

"Hanz has opened the store. It will not be long now."

The line inched forward. Everyone was sweating in the damp heat.

I saw the Bosun's mate coming down the passageway carrying two cartons of cigarettes and two bottles of vodka. He had rank. He stopped and spoke to Andre in Spanish. He smiled to me. The ship rolled again and threw him against the bulkhead.

He spoke again to Andre; pointed to his eye; and gestured at me.

I looked at Andre inquisitively.

"He said that you have first watch and should not drink until after it. He will come and get you a few minutes before you are to begin. You have the four to eight."

I didn't understand.

Andre leaned over and shouted in my ear "Wait until we are finished here. We will go to my cabin and I will explain everything."

We moved forward in the line until it was my turn. Hanz was sitting at a table inside the cabin with a ledger book in front of him. He looked up and saw me; and then looked back down at the ledger book and asked simply "What do you want?"

He looked up and clarified his question in his stilted German accent, "What would you like?"

He didn't like me. The First Mate had hired me. The old man from Roatan.

"You may have one bottle of liquor and two cartons of cigarettes. What would you like?"

A gray haired Spaniard was waiting behind Hanz for directions. I looked over at the cases of liquor and cigarettes stacked against the bulkhead. There were dozens and dozens of boxes of different brands of liquor and smokes.

Uh. Lets see. Do you have any Chardonnay? No? How about a nice Merlot? Oh. No huh. A quart of vodka will do. Cigarettes? Well. It's a nasty habit see. And I generally don't smoke because of the Surgeons' Generals warning and all; but since I'm going with the flow here; I think I'll take a carton of Winstons please. And put that on my tab; if you would. Thank you.

"One bottle of Smirnoff and a carton of Winstons, please."

Hanz looked over his shoulder at the Spaniard and spit out a few directions to him in Spanish. The Spaniard rifled through a couple of boxes and turned and handed me a quart bottle of vodka and a carton of Winston cigarettes.

I was in pig heaven.

Hanz never looked up.

I backed out of the cabin and Andre took my place. When he came out carrying his allotment; we both retreated like little kids to his cabin.

Andre stashed his bottle in a drawer underneath his bunk and stuck the cartons of cigarettes inside the smooth wooden rail of his sleeping compartment.

He had taped pictures of his family inside the area beneath the top bunk and had screwed a metal ashtray to the forward part of the wooden rail. Several books were stacked neatly on a homemade shelf he had made in the metal shop in the engine room. Most of the titles were in Spanish, but I could see a few in English.

It actually had a homey kind of feel to it. Comfortable. Personal. Lived in. I was in his house. I was a guest here. I felt welcomed for the first time in a long time.

He turned to me; took the bottle and cigarettes from my hands and set them on his bunk. He handed me a cigarette and gestured for me to sit in a chair that was shoved under a desk attached to the bulkhead at the foot of the bunks. He walked the few steps to the door of the cabin and closed it.

The noise level dropped considerably as Andre moved to his bunk and jumped up on it and sat. He lit his cigarette, turned to me, and smiled.

"We are at sea now. Things will run a little differently than when we are in port."

I leaned back in the chair and lit the cigarette. He had my full attention. He handed me an ashtray that was hidden in the lip of the bookshelf and continued.

"I will explain the watches first. There are only three sections of work on this ship. You are in the ship's gang. It is also called the deck crew. I am in the engineering department. I work on the generators, the engines, the pumps; so on. Miguel works in the galley. He is a member of the ship's mess."

"The Captain is in charge of all three departments. Willie Eubanks is in charge of the gang and all things which occur in regard to the cargo or maintenance while we are in port. And as First Mate, he is also a navigator while we are at sea."

"Riley is the Chief Engineer. He is in charge of the engine room and all things that occur in there. Hanz is the cook. He is in charge of the galley and the ship's store. He is the quartermaster as well."

"Do you understand so far?"

I nodded in the affirmative.

It was starting to fall together.

Andre took a long drag on his cigarette and continued.

"Carmen is the Bosun's Mate; and technically; he is your boss. He is your jefe' although any of the ship's officers may give you an order regardless of the department you work in. Sometimes you will work in other departments if someone is injured or sick; or if they need extra help; but Carmen is your boss and you should do as he tells you."

"In port we work eight hour shifts. You worked yesterday from eight until five, with one hour for lunch. At sea you will work four hours at a time. In your case; since you have the first watch from four until eight; you will work this evening from four until eight."

"It is simple, no?"

"And then at four in the morning; Carmen will wake you for your next watch. You will work from four until eight in the morning. Do you understand how this will work?"

I nodded again in the affirmative and Andre smiled and said "Good... good."

"Carmen or Miguel will relieve you briefly so that you may eat the meals which fall on your watch; but other than that Carmen does not work other than to ensure that you stand your watch at the given time. He will occasionally check the hatch covers over the hold; or the ballast tanks; but for the most part; his sole responsibility at sea is to ensure that you fulfill yours."

"He will wake you one half hour before your watch is to begin."

"He is a smart man with much experience. He can teach you much if you are willing to learn."

"When your watch is complete he will bring your replacement to relieve you. Since you are on the gang; your watch will be stood in the wheelhouse."

"It is clean work. You will probably enjoy it. The rest of the time at sea is yours to do with as you wish. You may sleep. Drink. Play cards. Masturbate. Read. You may do whatever you like. There is no where else to go, and little else to do."

"Now my young American friend; ask away."

"How many men are on this ship?"

"The Captain brought an assistant cook on this morning before we sailed; so in total; there are twenty-five souls on board."

"Eventually you will meet them all. It may seem like a large ship, but it will become very small very quickly. As for the other details...what can I tell you?"

"Why do the officers have a different dining hall than the crew?"

It was one of the first observations I had made after boarding the ship.

Andre paused; squashed his cigarette out in the ashtray and jumped to the floor. He walked to the porthole that was built into the bulkhead and looked out for a brief moment. He looked back at me and smiled as if to say... "That was a very good question."

He started playing with the porthole as he considered his answer.

The porthole was made of a heavy brass frame and a window made with a thick half inch circle of glass sealed inside it. The window was secured to the frame with heavy brass dogs that turned on screws.

Andre turned the dogs up and pulled them away from the frame. He swung the circular window open. It banged against the steel wall of the bulkhead with a heavy thunk. Andre secured it to the wall with another dog that was hanging from an eyelet welded to the steel.

"They eat in their own place; because as you have so obviously yet to learn; familiarity breeds contempt. That is why."

He stuck his head out the porthole and took a deep breathe of the fresh ocean air and turned back to me.

"Do not concern yourself with the world of officers. They are just as lonely as we are. It is enough that you and I have become friends."

I didn't quite understand. I liked the First Mate when I had met him. I had felt something toward him. I don't know what it was. Kinship maybe. I had only known Andre for the better part of a day and I already felt a strong friendship toward him.

Andre looked at his watch. "You have about two hours before they will expect you to work. I have the first watch also. Let's go on top and relax for a while."

We walked to my cabin and left my draw from the ship's store on my bunk. We meandered through the passageways; stopping briefly in each of the cabins that were open to meet the occupants. I didn't say much.

I just nodded and smiled; shook hands when they were offered. Most of them could not speak English so Andre made the introductions.

We made our way finally to the rear ladder well and climbed to the deck above the officer's mess. There were a few wooden chairs back here and Andre pulled one up; sat down, and kicked his feet up on the rail.

I walked up to the steel rail, leaned against it; and looked over and into the propeller wash. I let it hypnotize me.

Everything was happening so fast.

I couldn't go back now even if I wanted to.

The brief wave of nausea I had felt when we had left Government Cut and hit the open sea had left me. I had my sea legs now. The stern of the ship rose and fell in harmony with the swells.

How had I gotten here?

Where was I going?

What were they thinking?

I closed my eyes and wished my younger brother a happy birthday. He was somewhere out there in a world I had left behind.

Would he survive?

Would I ever see him again?

The horizon was filled with ocean. I was alone on an empty sea. Florida was somewhere to the west.

A wave of loneliness washed over me and left me dripping in guilt.

Chapter Ten

This planet has it's own identity. It is alive in its own unique way. Each of us who came to visit here so long ago developed our own unique identities in this place.

You are only beginning now to realize that the universe; much like this planet; is teeming with life at every turn and on every level. You are only now beginning to understand that everything; in some aspect; is alive.

You are only now beginning to suspect that all things originate from a single unified source.

In your savage and limited understandings; in your fragile and archaic dogmas; you have believed for centuries that your race and this planet is the center of the universe.

I am 702 years old by your counting.

500 years ago in your counting this planet was flat.

Or so your species believed.

You were mistaken then. You are mistaken now.

Your understanding about many things is about to change.

You cannot stop the shift that comes.

We could not stop it.

Nor can you.

Our single great mistake was that as a race; we were overtaken by the same beauty of this place that overtakes all human beings. We slowly forgot who we were and why we had come here in the first.

Our technology allowed us to live well beyond the life-span of other human beings who inhabited this earth.

Our technology permitted us things in our coming; that in our fleeing we are now forever denied.

We came here; and planted seeds here; long before we ourselves ventured here.

Just as a gardener first experiments by planting seeds in fertile soil; so too did we. We did not know ourselves which seeds would grow.

We wanted to see which ones would thrive.

It does not matter in this moment.

You don't have to look very hard to see the truth of this.

Just as you dismiss our ancient existence; so too; will you dismiss the explanation of theirs.

To know that you are descended from apes is a greater comfort to the many of you. To know the truth; is to know that you are descended from our seed. To know that truth is to know your Origin.

To know your Origin is to remember ours.

To our great surprise; in our lengthy absence; the seeds that we had planted; each of them had flourished. Some more than others. But they had all flourished.

The primitive human-like creatures that had evolved slowly over millions of years on this planet were overtaken by the offspring of the seeds we had planted.

Of all the colors of men on this earth; there is only one truly native to this place. The rest have been transplanted here from other places to see how they would grow.

They were all pioneers.

All of them came here of their own free will.

They were left here with only one tool.

They were given one simple principle that allowed them to persevere and survive. It is the only tool you possess as a species.

We will not give you anymore.

You have misused the one we gave you.

The natives of this world never discovered this principle.

To this day; the few natives who still remain still do not understand it.

Your scientists cannot explain its appearance.

When we returned; we came as teachers; but we became like Gods to those we had planted here.

That was not our intent.

In our arrogance we began to feel superior to those we had returned in time to teach. We labor in servitude to the universe now as compensation for that.

They were like children to us.

We did not know that in the eyes of the universe; the student is as great as the teacher.

This was our lesson.

Instead; they became like slaves to us.

In truth; that was never our intent. But it became so.

We were seduced ourselves. We fell victim to the same seductions; the same illusions; that you yourselves are fallen victims to.

But we knew it; and we ignored it.

In our end; we were punished for it.

We took this planet's indifference and silence as our permission to do as we wished while we were here.

That was an error. Our species exists as proof of it.

It was our downfall.

We took this planet's quiet majesty as our license to do as we liked in any manner, shape, or form; regardless of the consequences we were inviting.

The beauty of this world; its awe-inspiring, indulgent nature beguiled us just as it has beguiled you.

I have said enough for now. I will leave it for Tesla. She would try to explain what has happened to us in a way that Davitch will comprehend.

I will listen as she begins to speak.

Her eloquence is beautiful in its simplicity.

She uses many of the symbols taken from your world to communicate the events which led to the Deluge.

It is far more complex than her simple explanation; but we had a great sea to cross before we could show Davitch the submerged ruins of our first coming. He had much to learn before we entered those waters.

I have said enough. So I will listen for a while.

Davitch has had nothing to say.

He is in a new dimension. He hovers near Tesla like a newborn. Tesla is speaking to him to comfort the fear he is feeling in this strange and unfamiliar world. It will take him some time for him to adjust to his new surroundings.

127

It is time for us to go.

We have said our last farewells to Mara at the edge of the lagoon and we are headed eastward into the ocean toward the Appa Sea. Sallon is nowhere to be heard. He is gone forever from this place.

There would be no sound of his voice. I would listen many years for it.

The wasted ruins of our ancient cities lie on the sunken continent of our forgotten race. It is many moons away.

I can sense that Tesla is falling in love. No. The truth of it is, is that Tesla has already fallen in love.

Ebron and Neva can sense it as well.

Tesla makes me snicker. Her choice of images as she started to explain did not fit the size of the task that she has undertaken.

Explaining how we came to be is not as simple as a fly on an elephant's ass. I smile inside as she begins.

"Davitch?"

"Yes, Tesla."

"Do you know how big an elephant is?"

"Yes. Is this a riddle, Tesla?"

"No. Just listen to me. I will try to explain a concept to you. It will make it easier to explain other things. Until you completely learn our language; I must communicate with you in images you will understand. Is this acceptable to you?"

"I love you, too; Tesla." Davitch said quietly.

So Tesla began.

The sun chased across the sky to the west as the pod made its way deeper into the Atlantic. Soon the island and the lagoon disappeared from the horizon.

Soon Davitch became lost as Tesla flooded him with her words.

"An elephant is an elephant," she began. And the words mixed with the waves...

I snickered.

"Stop that!"

Tesla was snickering too. She knew how funny she sounded.

"He doesn't know that he is an elephant." continued Tesla....

I snickered again.

"Yes he does. Stuff him in conch shell and see if he doesn't know he's not an elephant!"

Snicker snicker snicker....

"Eden! Please."

Now Tesla was laughing. I could hear her playful snicker...

"Oh... alright! But it's going to be a long swim!" snicker snicker snicker...

Davitch was snickering too....

"He only knows that he is. He only knows that he is like other elephants because he eats what they eat and looks like they look. He wanders with other elephants and mates with other elephants and lives out his life and dies with other elephants without ever questioning the fact that he is an elephant."

"He never wakes up one morning and thinks to himself, Why am I an elephant? He is just happy being an elephant."

"Ok., Tesla. Lets' see if Davitch is conscious. Is he awake? If he is like most humans, he's probably still in shock. Is his mind intact?"

It was. Tesla knew it was. She was in it. Holding it gently.

"Now. Every so often a fly lands on the elephant. The fly is just a fly and the fly doesn't live long enough or have a brain big enough to know anything much about anything. It is just happy being a fly."

"But the fly wants to do two things. No matter how big or small it's brain is; the fly only wants to do two things."

"I'm hungry, Tesla. I want to eat!"

"Eden...."

Snicker...snicker...snicker......

"It wants to survive and it wants to reproduce. It doesn't even know that it wants to do these two things. It is more instinct than thought. The fly is nature."

"The elephant wants to survive and reproduce. Just like the fly. All living things want to survive and reproduce."

"The elephant doesn't think much about the fly. The fly is so tiny and the elephant is so big."

"Anyway; the fly is hungry and wants to survive. So the fly bites the elephant. To the fly, the elephant is food. To the elephant, the fly is nuisance."

"The fly is so tiny and the bite is so small that the elephant barely notices the fly biting it. But just because the elephant lets the fly bite it; it doesn't mean that the elephant doesn't feel it. It just means that the elephant has more important things to do than swat the fly."

"So the fly goes away and mates and has a bunch of babies. The babies are hungry. They want to survive too; and eventually they will want to reproduce as well. So they look for the elephant. The elephant just wants to be."

"One fly biting the elephant won't hurt it. Two flies biting the elephant won't hurt it. But enough flies biting the elephant at the same time can drop the elephant and kill it."

"This is where the brain of the elephant begins to think. The fly isn't thinking at all. He is too busy eating. He is too busy surviving. He is too busy reproducing. But the elephant. He's bigger. He lives longer. His brain is equipped for more than just survival. He begins to experience his existence on a new level simultaneously with his desire to survive and reproduce."

"The flies have become a problem for him. They have begun to threaten his survival. He needs to find a solution to that threat. His problem is not that the flies are hungry. Flies are always hungry, Davitch. His problem is not that there are too many of them. There are always too many flies."

"Part of the elephant's problem is that the flies are greedy, mindless creatures driven by instinct. They don't care if they kill the elephant. Most mindless creatures do not care if they kill the host upon which they feed. Flies are like a virus."

"The elephant cares. Of course he cares. But the flies don't care."

"They don't care because they are insulated from the consequences of their actions by the elephant's indifference."

"Another part of the elephant's problem is that he has no way to communicate to the flies the threat the flies have become to him. The elephant doesn't hate the flies. He doesn't hate them yet. He doesn't hate them until they become a threat to his existence. Hate is really a poor choice of word. It is more a word of priority. It is a word of survival. Fittest. That is a good word. Who is fittest?"

"He has no way to warn them that he has begun to think on a new level of understanding. The elephant thinks on several levels. The flies think on only one. This is survival of species, Davitch."

"In addition to reproduction and survival; the flies have added another dimension to the elephant's existence. They have made the elephant think in a new way. The flies have made the elephant think in way that he never thought before."

"The elephant is no longer peacefully co-existing with the flies on a sublime level of survival and reproduction."

"The flies; in their mindless greed; have added to the elephant's thinking the new dimensions of fear and pain."

"Now the elephant is driven by his desire to survive; and he is also motivated to action by his pain; and so now the elephant adds to his thinking a new dimension; the dimension of fear. In his pain his fear emerges in it."

"Self-preservation; the urge to survive; kicks in. The elephant decides that he will take care of the flies. He will drop the flies before they drop him. The elephant decides to kill the flies."

"The elephant begins to fear the things he knows can kill it. He begins to hate the things he fears. So he sets out to kill the things he fears."

"The flies will never see it coming. Their brains are not that big."

"Nature has taught the elephant slowly over time what he must do. The elephant does not run madly about. He walks slowly. He walks slowly so that the swarm of flies follows his big, swaying ass. He never lets them know that anything is different or about to change. He just wanders on over to the watering hole."

"The swarm of flies never sees the elephant's explosive moment. They never see what the elephant has in his mind."

"In one lazy, pain-filled moment; in one casual, lumbering roll; the elephant bathes in the mud of the watering hole; killing most; if not all of the flies that are too fat with his blood to fly."

"It is intended, Davitch. It is not accidental. It looks natural. But it is intentional. The elephant survives because nature intends him to. He survives because he is an elephant; he is not a fly."

"Are you a fly, Davitch; or are you an elephant?"

"I don't know what I am anymore, Tesla."

That was good. Let us see if the human child had grasped these concepts. Reproduction and Survival. Pain. Fear. It was a good start. Tesla was a teacher. This is what we had come here to do. It is a sadness that we had forgotten why we had come. There was so much to learn. So much to teach.

It was a good start. Tesla was a good teacher. She was patient. She loved Davitch. I could hear it in her way with him. He was a good student. He did not interrupt. He was following her every word; her every move.

His first night in the ocean would be interesting.

He would not sleep his first or second night. We would need to pace ourselves for him until he learned this skill. The sun would set soon.

Tesla continued

"Take the ocean, Davitch."

"It gives and it takes."

"It's secret is not such a secret. It's secret is so obvious that no one but those of us who live in it can see it. It is a source. It is alive. It ebbs and it flows."

"But it is a timeless place. Few live long enough to see it's timelessness. If there is a secret to it; it is this. The secret is to be there when it is giving; and hopefully; to be absent when it is taking. It has no prejudice. It does not care; it does not consider; and it gives no matter to your age, to your race, to your species, to your gender, to your station in life when it gives or when it takes."

"It can not be killed. It has an intelligence bigger than that of the fly. Do you understand?"

"This planet is a planet of water. It is a blue planet. This planet is a planet of oceans. Is this lost to you?"

"If the oceans die, Davitch. We all perish. Do you see this?"

"Yes Tesla. I think I understand. But I am not sure how this matters to me. I am taken away. I do not know what to say. I only know what I feel in this moment. I am lost. I am lost. It is as though I am alive in a different life with a memory of another. How can this be?"

"I was wondering when you would ask me this."

"Davitch. It is not as complicated as you would make it seem. All life is one. You are threatened by the loss of what you knew. You are threatened by the loss of what you think you knew. But I tell you; they are dreams. They are only dreams."

"My world is no more real than yours."

"We are here only to play for a little while and dream this dream.

And then we must answer the call of our source and return to it. Like a child returning to his mother's call at the end of a very long day."

"Eden's mother Ama was taken with no thought given to the fact that she was Keeper of Our Way."

"My mother and father were both taken from it."

"We are all of us; orphaned in our way."

"But the ocean is like a mother to us all. It will love us, and it will scold us. But it will never forsake us. We all are dependent on it."

"It is like everything else upon this planet. It is like so many other things your species does not understand. Every action has a consequence. Every bottle has a genie that can grant a wish or inflict a curse. Every dawn has a sunset." "Every tide has a wash. Something comes and something goes." "Something is given and; like you; Davitch; something must be taken."

"But it is like this only here. There is nowhere else in the universe where it is so. This planet is the only place in the universe where it is like this. That is why we have remained here.

To remind you.

We have remained for the coming of the shift."

"You are to be a part of it."

"I am to be a part of it."

"It is a wonderful time to be alive."

"We lost so many of our people during the Deluge."

"It was a grievous time for us. The memory of that single day is embedded in the consciousness of your species."

"It came upon us in one day. No one saw it coming. One moment we were as we were. In the next moment we were as refugees."

"Such is the elephant. We were the fly."

"The elephant did not run to the waterhole. We did not see it coming."

"He turned and rolled."

"We did not see it coming."

"We see it now."

"We look back and see it now."

"But I cannot see it, Tesla. I am so lost. I am...I do not belong in your world."

"No Davitch. You belong in our world as much as we belong in yours.

You are as much a part of our world as we are a part of yours. We are inseparable. Our world is as inseparable from yours as yours is from ours. Your race descended from ours. We are one."

"You are so much a child."

"You have so much to learn."

"Tesla. If I am so much a child...how is that I have come now to wander in this place with you?"

"That is not your question to ask; nor my question to answer, Davitch."

"Why does the elephant seek his own survival?"

"You are greater than the fly. You are greater than the elephant."

"What is the next level of understanding beyond the elephant's fear and pain, Davitch? Tell me. What does the elephant feel beyond his fear and pain?"

"Love? What else is there to feel?"

"Yes. Love. Beyond that. There is nothing else to feel. The elephant feels love. He loves the sun. He loves his mate."

"He loves the savannahs. He loves the cool of the shade. He loves his brood. He loves his play. He does not hate. He loves his existence in the rise and fall of the sun."

"Beyond that there is nothing but love."

"But he is not a man."

"He is not dolphin."

"He is only elephant."

"He can feel love. But beyond that he has no way of expressing it. He does not paint. He does not write. He does not build. He does not compose music. He eats grass and defecates. He is animal."

"He is nature."

"What have you created, Davitch? What song have you sang? What prayer have you prayed? Do you believe beyond your own existence? Do you need to?"

"That is what makes you greater than the elephant. It is what makes you greater than the fly."

"But I have done none of these things, Tesla."

"But you have, Davitch. But you have."

"Your presence among us is proof of that."

"No prayer goes unanswered. No plea goes unheard.. You are here because somewhere; somehow; something; something heard your keening in the vast emptiness of the great ocean and decided that you should be answered."

"Do not believe for a moment that you are here with us by accident. If that were the case; than there is no order to the universe and everything is madness and we are all insane. And there is nothing but silence and darkness beyond our lives here."

"You are here for a reason."

"You will be a father by the child in my womb. Tell me now that there is no reason to that. I carry your son inside me. Tell me of your feeling about it."

"Would you that he be born in the sand? Would you that he be born in the world of men? You have not yet seen our world. How can you answer the questions I pose? How can you tell me of your feelings in this when you cannot tell me how you yourself feel in our world?"

"Tell me how the elephant feels when the fly bites his ass."

"Davitch."

"Tell me you do not love me."

"Tell me now."

"I cannot. Tesla. I am in love with you."

"You have answered my question, Davitch. What name shall we give our son?"

Night fell.

The summer storm swept like a heavy whicker broom upon them from the west. It beat them in quick, pummeling welts of rain and hail.

Tesla took Davitch to the depths. Breathe deep deep, she said. Hold it. You can hold it forever.

We can. We have held our breath for centuries.

Neva and Ebron took sides upon them. Eden watched from afar.

It was a double edged sword that tested the choice Eden had made. The man-child had only one day in the ocean. He had not learned to eat nor sleep in the swells.

By morning of the following day; he had tired to the point where he was near foundering. The pod slowed to a stop. They would rest, play; and feed.

Tesla would make love to him.

It would restore his strength.

He was young as dolphins aged. He would age quickly enough.

They had entered the waters of the great whites.

Now they were prey themselves.

There were too few of them to be a formidable deterrent to any kind of pack assault. They would need to move quickly through these waters; tired or not.

Davitch would need to reach deep and pull hard or he would perish in this journey. There was no mercy to be found here.

There was no sense in asking for it.

The great whites were a perfected; mindless, killing machine that had evolved seamlessly through the centuries.

They were older than time itself.

There was no bargain to be had with them.

Davitch was an easy prey. He was young. He was weak. He was confused.

The pod would stretch to protect him.

We would do well to avoid any encounter with them. I could hear Ebron's echoes. I could hear Neva's as well.

The Great whites did not have this skill. They are fish. We could avoid them. They are blind and deaf and dumb.

But they desire to survive and reproduce.

We are food to them.

Tesla did not tell Davitch what we were against.

We can see a pea in its pod. We can see a grain of sand on a shell. We can move as few creatures move through the water. So fine is our sense; that we can see in the dark the things you cannot see.

The bones that have been broken.

The illnesses that will not heal.

These are the things you cannot see.

These are the things that are given us to see.

The things that you cannot.

We were in water so deep we could not feel the bottom.

The chasm.

It is the edge of the place where our continent lies.

It is the edge of the place where your continent begins.

The moon was hidden that first night behind a black sky of thunder heads that rolled the ocean over and under itself. We hid beneath the mountainous waves; taking our breath in leisurely intervals between the roller coaster ride of the swells.

Davitch said he found the storm exciting. His proximity to Tesla spoke otherwise; we could sense his fear and felt a bit of sorrow for him.

It is a playful thing to us.

The waves are indeed a joy to ride when stirred to such a height.

He will learn. He will see.

He was such a pup.

But we did not take it from him.

We left it to him.

He was frightened in it. The waves were ferocious.

They gave us camouflage in our journey.

We made two suns passing in the storm.

We passed through a huge belt of mackerel during it. Davitch would have gone hungry were it not for Tesla's pity.

Though he tried; he was hopelessly inexperienced.

Ebron and Neva stuffed themselves; skillfully herding; the fish running to each other in a maddening race to escape one hungry dolphin from another.

Personally; I don't care much for mackerel. I prefer orange ruffie; grouper; red snapper; or tarpon.

Davitch took the mackerel from Tesla without hesitation.

She loves him so much. He was hungry. He loves her. He loves all of us.

In such short a time; too.

Chapter Eleven

"I am the worthless; shiftless lying mess within your happiness."
"I will become the truth-filled product of your empty hallowedness."

Andre knew where I was. He had been there in his own way as well. One of the beautiful things about the sea is that it gives a man plenty of room and plenty of time to look inside himself.

Andre had done his own share of soul searching.

In a way; he had started out much like me; by running. As a boy; he had made his way from his birthplace in Blue Fields, Nicaragua to Managua. The poverty of Blue Fields crushed everything.

So he ran.

He couldn't remember the exact date of his birthday. He had eventually purchased his identity papers. That was how young he had been when he left. He had lived on the streets of Managua for several years alternately begging and stealing before he managed to stow away on a cargo ship bound for the United States.

The crew of the vessel had found him huddling in an empty Conex box. They beat him viciously when they first discovered him, and rather than return to Managua and lose the three days they had made; they decided to turn him over to the U.S. Immigration authorities when they reached Miami.

Andre had jumped ship and ran before the Immigration Officers had boarded the vessel for port inspection. He was just a kid. He didn't matter.

He was about 24 years old now.

He had returned to Blue Fields two years earlier in search of his parents. He found them in the same corrugated tin shack they had been living in when he had left.

One his brothers had died of influenza the year before. The blinding, abject poverty his family was still living in made him weep. He had left with no desire to ever return again.

He sent his mother money at Christmas. That was the only real concession he made to his past. He did not like to dwell there and he did not like to speak of it. It was a painful place for him. I would respect that.

He had picked up the ship a year earlier after he had been fired from the Empress for fraternizing with a young blond from New Jersey. The blond had been on her honeymoon with her new husband. The way he told it; she seduced him. They had been caught. He had been fired.

The ship was in port the same day as the Empress. A short walk and a short talk and he was working again.

Andre had learned to speak fluent, immaculate English working on the cruise ships. It was his dream to marry an American and become an American citizen. My only observation to him was that perhaps he should begin with women who weren't already married. He laughed at my remark.

"Yes. I suppose you are right." he said smiling. "It would simplify matters greatly."

He barely had an accent.

Andre loved to read. It was something we both had in common. He had read a wide range of material. Everything from western novels to complicated books by Nietze and Gurdjeff.

I listened as he rambled.

I felt like I was being swept away by the most recent events. Everything was out of my control. Nothing seemed to fit. It couldn't get any stranger than this. Or so I thought.

A week ago I was doing homework for my ninth grade teachers. A week ago I was getting high under the bleachers behind the high school. A week ago I was playing kissy face with Melody; pinning her aggressively against her wall locker while copping feels of her breasts through her blouse.

A week ago? A day ago? It seemed like a lifetime ago.

What were they doing now?

Did anybody miss me? Did anybody even notice I was gone?

Questions. I was haunted by a thousand questions.

Andre and I talked until Carmen came to get me. He had been drinking and had a cheery buzz going. He pointed at his eye and gestured for me to follow him. I nodded goodbye to Andre and left silently with the Bosun's Mate.

We walked across the expanse of deck forward to the wheelhouse. Carmen pointed to the doorway which opened into the bridge and turned and headed back aft. I climbed the ladder to the bridge and knocked loudly at the door.

The First Mate bellowed loudly from inside. "Entra!"

I entered and when he saw that it was me he smiled. I shut the door nervously behind me.

A quick look around told me this was no place for jokes or horseplay. This was the cleanest; and in a strikingly beautiful; surreal way; the prettiest part of the ship.

The bridge occupied the top portion of the forecastle and was filled with windows. You could look in any direction and see the horizon twenty miles away.

Everything in the Wheelhouse was trimmed in oak or brass

A large spoked wheel half the height of a man and decorated with polished brass rings dominated the center of the bridge.

A huge solid oak table slanting like a drafting desk rested against a bank of windows situated directly behind the wheel. Directly above it was an enormous storage shelf divided into pigeon holes stuffed with navigational charts. There were hundreds of frayed paper charts stacked one upon the other.

Tacked to the table was a chart of the lower east coast of Florida. Laying on the chart were pencils, a compass; slide rule, ruler; and inside an open red velvet lined mahogany box set to one side was a beautifully polished solid brass sextant.

A bank of VHF radios lay directly underneath the chart table. There was a Loran Satellite Array Console attached to a hooded radar unit standing like a midget sentry next to the helmsman; who stood like a sentry himself; hands at the wheel.

A phone to the engine room hung on the wall next to the chart table and a sold brass; dual handled change station marked with full ahead; half ahead; slow; stop; half astern; full astern; waited silently beside it.

The dual handles of the station were resting in the notched position of Full Ahead. Mark speed was chalked onto a board above the wheel and said 7 Knots.

A solid oak sitting table on the port side of the bridge sat with heavy porcelain cups and a fresh pot of coffee. Hanging from hooks from three sets of windows were high powered binoculars. The entire wheelhouse was lit with banks of florescent lighting and next to them were banks of red florescent lights for night running.

A plushly upholstered Captain's chair stood next to the Chart table. It was bolted to the floor. It made me briefly think of the T.V. chairs in the Greyhound bus station.

In front of the wheel and slanted toward the helmsman was a glass encased floating compass marked elaborately with the cardinal points of North, South, East, and West. The 360 degrees were cleanly spaced and marked in thick black lines a quarter of an inch long.

There was a soft green glow that seemed to originate from underneath the compass housing and flow up under and into it.

The entire room was paneled beneath the windows in oak wainscot and the floor was highly polished in one inch oak strips.

Sheepskin rain skins hung at both entrances to the bridge.

The place was gorgeous and all I could do was gawk.

The First Mate spoke to the helmsman in Spanish and the helmsman reached over to the bulkhead and pulled an intricately spliced length of half inch line up and tied the wheel into a fixed position. He left quietly as the First Mate turned to me.

"Step to the wheel and put your hand to it." he said

I stepped forward and assumed a standing position similar to the one I had observed from the man who had just departed the bridge.

I turned to the First Mate as if to say "You mean like this?"

He stepped up behind me and repositioned my hands so they were equidistant on two of the upward spokes. He pointed to the compass floating serenely floating in the glass case in front of me and began to explain.

"We are on a course which will take us South along the coast of Florida. When we reach a point that is approximately 50 miles north of Cuba; we will head South by Southwest across the Gulf of Mexico. When we reach the Yucatan Peninsula; we will take on a Pilot in a place called Progresso for the coastal waters."

"We will then head to a small place called Los Colorados to load salt. Our current heading is 180 degrees."

He pointed to the needle on the compass and explained to me that I should keep the compass point aligned with the numerical value marked on the bezel of the compass.

I nodded silently in the affirmative.

"So this is how it works." I thought to myself.

"Pay attention and keep the ship headed into the direction I've showed you. You screw up; and you'll be swimming back to Miami."

Little did I know. He didn't say it in a mean way. It was a gentle gruff. He smiled when he said it. I took no offense. I would pay attention. I would do this job. I wouldn't give him any reason to complain or criticize.

I watched as he untied the clove hitch that held the wheel in place. He let the line fall back in place against the bulkhead and stepped back.

I played the wheel briefly to get a feel for it and found the ship to be amazingly responsive to any change in control. I could actually feel the ship turn under my hand. The change of direction was more pronounced on the bow than on the stern.

"Are you finished playing now?" His voice had deepened.

"Keep it on 180 degrees and don't go wandering off on me."

That pretty much set the tone of my standing watch in the wheelhouse my first day at sea.

It was serious business; steering and navigating the ship. A couple of degrees off course could put us miles off our route.

The First Mate spent the rest of the watch slowly explaining the workings of the ship; and I after I began to feel a little more at ease; I began to ask questions.

The Bosun's Mate sent Miguel up to the wheelhouse at six to relieve me for twenty minutes for dinner. Miguel also brought a tray with the First Mate's dinner on it for him.

I bolted back to the crew mess and ate the leftovers that sat in covered dishes on the main stove. When I was finished; I put my dishes in the deep sink and hiked back up to the wheelhouse.

Miguel stood to the side and let me resume my watch. The First Mate had eaten and Miguel took his tray as he left.

I kept the wheel on 180 degrees. The sun was slowly beginning to fall in the west. It would be my first night at sea. The air was warm and the sea was calm.

I watched as the sun slowly began to sink into the ocean.

Florida was somewhere out there.

The queer who had tried to hustle me on Biscayne Boulevard was out there.

The Customs Officer was out there.

My world...my younger brother was out there.

I fell into a silence that was as deep as the ocean itself.

The First Mate noticed that I had fallen silent and thoughtful.

He took the sextant out on the flying bridge to take several shots before the sun finally set. Maybe he was just giving me a few moments to be alone with my thoughts. Maybe.

I had the steering down. If there was anything out the ordinary; the First Mate was within earshot.

The Captain was sleeping. We had left Miami without a Second Mate so both the First Mate and the Captain would be standing eight hour shifts until they could find a Licensed Mate who could navigate.

I watched the spectacle of the sunset from the bridge and could not believe the difference in a sunset at sea.

Everything became brilliantly green and then blue just before the corona of the sun dipped below the horizon. The afterglow lasted for about twenty minutes and then night came and it was dark.

The stars started to flicker on one at a time; and soon the sky was full of them. The First Mate reentered the wheelhouse and pointed out a few constellations for me. Then he sat down in the Captain's chair and began to do some calculations.

He watched the Bosun's mate stumbling up the deck toward the wheelhouse with Frank and chuckled. "Here come's your relief, boy."

He looked at his watch and mumbled that we were making good way.

I would be relieved in a few minutes. I would meet the Captain on my next watch.

Frank entered the wheelhouse and set a coffee can down at his feet.

He took the wheel from my hands; spit in the can; and asked me the heading.

It was the first time I had ever seen a man spit like that. It was like a dog taking a dump. It was a handful of spit.

"The heading." he asked again.

"Uh..180 Degrees."

"Thank you. You are relieved."

He turned his head and spit into the can again. He didn't look at me. He just turned the wheel a few times back and forth to check its response and began to search the horizon.

I left the bridge by the way I had come. The first mate was taking shots with the sextant again using the stars this time. Maybe he was just killing time. He brought it down from his eye when I exited the bridge.

"Good night, sir." I said as I stepped to the ladder well.

"Good night, son." he replied.

"Hey, boy."

I turned at the ladder head and paused. "Sir?"

"You did good. Keep it up."

"Yes sir. Thank you sir. I'll do my best."

The First Mate smiled and said simply; "You do just that."

I hopped, skipped, and danced back to the aft castle across a deck that was rolling slowly back and forth. I had my sealegs good now and I felt good. It was almost as if I belonged. The starlit sky was overpowering and I felt dizzy looking up into it.

This wasn't so bad.

I climbed the aft castle ladder and went to look for Andre.

Andre had already been relieved and was in his cabin getting ready to shower. He was filthy. He smiled at me through the dirt and his pearly white teeth stood out and made the dirt almost comical. He reminded me of Pigpen from a Peanuts cartoon.

"Wait for me in my cabin."

I walked in and sat down in the desk chair. I could hear Andre above the thrum thrum thrum of the ship's engines singing a song from some Elton John album.."Someone saved my life tonight...coulda been...coulda been.."

I got up and walked over to his bunk and looked at the titles again. I was starved for something to read. Maybe he would loan me one of them?

I had eight hours before my next watch and I was already wondering what I was going to do with myself.

I could see an English version of the King James Bible and next to it a Spanish version of the same bible. Andre had a couple of books on Maritime law; one by Erich From called the ART OF LOVING; a few by Hemingway; Huxley; Buck; and others that I didn't recognize. In all there was a tidy library with a decent selection.

When he emerged from the head he walked into the cabin and dropped his towel and reached into the drawer beneath his bunk for a clean pair of shorts.

His skin was a light bronze and I noticed then that there were thin lines across his back that were lighter than the rest of his skin. Andre turned and noticed that I had been staring.

I didn't have to ask.

"Oh. Those. When I was a boy in Managua; I was caught stealing from a shopkeeper. He turned me over to the police. The beat me and then whipped me until I lost consciousness. Then they woke me up; shaved my head; and turned me loose."

"If you should ever happen to wander the streets of Managua; take caution when you see a bald headed child. They are little thieves who will steal the watch from your wrist or the wallet from your hip. Do not turn your back on them."

I turned away. I was embarrassed. Andre had his own share of scars.

I guess we all do.

It's just that for some of us the scars may be on the inside rather than on the outside.

Andre dressed and pulled the bottle of vodka from his drawer. He sent me to the galley for some orange juice and glasses

When I returned; he cracked the bottle open and poured a generous amount of vodka in both glasses and mixed in some orange juice. He took one of the glasses and I apologized for the lack of ice.

"Life is so primitive here. We must make do with what we have."

Now that I thought about it; I hadn't seen any ice yet while I had been on the ship. There was the deep freezer; but only Hanz had keys to it.

It sounded like another simple cruelty.

"Andre. Could I ask a favor of you?"

"Make it a small one my young American friend. For I am as poor as you."

"Teach me to speak Spanish, Andre; like you speak English?"

He thought for a moment and then smiled.

"Ah; to speak Spanish is a very difficult thing. Spanish is a very beautiful language and requires a passionate heart to learn. Do you have a passionate heart? Yes. I believe you do. So yes. My answer is yes. I will help you to learn it."

He reached up to his book shelf and pulled down the English and Spanish versions of the King James bible from their perch and handed them to me.

"You can read? Yes. Of course you can read. How stupid of me to ask."

"For the matter of textbooks; these will have to suffice. But between these and the practice we will have; you will learn quickly."

Andre quickly reviewed the three basic conjugations of the verbs in Spanish.

He pointed out that on the ship there were at least three different dialects of Spanish to practice in. Willy Eubanks; the First Mate; and Arturo were both from British Honduras and spoke a dialect that was native to the Island of Roatan. Miguel was Mexican.

Andre spoke Spanish from Nicaragua and he also spoke Portugese; which is also very common in Central and South America.

There were several other Mexicans on board so I should have many willing instructors. Carmen was from Honduras.

Hanz was German but also spoke the European dialect of Spanish known as Castillian. He spoke German, naturally; but was also fluent in Vietnamese.

Riley; the Chief Engineer spoke English and Patua. He also spoke Tagalo; which was a hybrid of Spanish and Portugese spoken mostly in the Philippines.

All in all, there was a tower of babble of languages on the ship enough to generally confuse the hell out of me.

Andre stuffed his dirty clothes into a nylon mesh bag and led us up to the afterdeck above the officer's mess. He tied a half-inch line around the neck of the bag and threw it overboard into the turbulent wash of the propellers. He slowly payed out the line until the bag bounced and hopped in the wake a hundred yards behind the ship. He tied the line off to the rail; pulled up one of the wooden chairs and sat down, kicking his feet up as he did.

I looked at him and back at the bag bouncing in the wake.

I had to laugh.

"What are you doing?"

"What does it look like I am doing? I am doing my laundry."

He smiled and shook his head. "Of course. How would you know?"

"I will let the bag bounce in the wake for three hours or so and then I will pull it in. I'll take it into the head and rinse the salt water out of it and hang them in there to dry. Then I will have clean clothes. Simple; yes?"

"While we are at sea; fresh water is limited to cooking and bathing. If Hanz catches you washing your clothes in fresh water; he will find a way to punish you for it. Everyone does it this way. If you wish to have clean clothes at sea; you must do it this way."

"Actually it does a fair job."

It was an eery sight.

I could see the bag of laundry bouncing in the night under a starlit sky in the white foam of the wake. It looked like Andre was trolling for some huge creature of the deep using his laundry as bait. I wondered what great ocean quarry would strike on a greasy bag of dirty clothes.

The horizon stretched out until it faded into blackness. I counted dozens of shooting stars falling tragically though the atmosphere.

The blackness of the Carribean night devoured them and each wish I made upon them as they fell. We drank our vodka and orange juice quietly as the laundry bounced in the wash.

Somewhere on the western horizon; we could see the red; green; and white of a ship in the distance. Andre estimated that it was maybe fifteen miles away. It looked tiny, like a child's toy bobbing in the dark a hands' breadth away. It disappeared as quickly as it had appeared.

We would see several more that evening. Always in the distance.

Never close enough to make out what type of vessel it was although Andre suggested that they might be either cargo vessels like ours, or cruise ships, as both used this route with regular frequency.

We were lit up ourselves. Green and red running lights illuminated the port and starboard running wells. A subdued light from a few exterior deck lights and cabin lights fell over the sides of the ship and cascaded into the impenetrable black depths below.

A white stern light indicated to any ship which saw us which way we were pointed. We were headed into the maw of the gulf.

Every now and then the water would glimmer with a sparkling ephemeral light; as if to signal to the ship that something from the deep had noted and acknowledged its passing.

We talked and drank while I butchered and practiced my Spanish with Andre. Andre would point at something; pronounce the word in Spanish; and I would repeat it several times; trying to mimic his accent as closely as possible.

The evening passed quickly.

An hour or so before midnight; Andre hauled his laundry in from the ocean. We took it down to the head and rinsed it in fresh water. He decided since the evening was warm and the weather was good that he would use the same line he used to wash it; to hang his laundry on the afterdeck.

I called it a night and retired to my cabin with the bibles to read.

I awoke to the Bosun's mate gently shaking me awake. It was dark in the cabin and Carmen reached over my head and turned the bunk light on above my head. I climbed out of my bunk and dressed quickly.

I made a quick trip to the head; washed my face; and followed the Bosun's mate out into the early morning darkness. He brought me as far as the ladder to the forecastle; pointed; and returned the way he came.

I climbed slowly up the ladder; taking in the view of the ocean as I did.

When I entered the bridge; the man on watch turned and silently nodded to me. I immediately took his place; asked for the heading which had remained unchanged; and felt the wheel once again in my hands.

The First Mate was preparing to end his watch. He came up to me and spoke briefly.

"Captain McLean is taking the next watch. He's a good man. Keep a good eye out and don't fall asleep."

He turned and left as the Captain of the ship walked through the hatch.

"Good morning, son. Steady as she goes."

"Yes sir. 180 degrees."

The Captain was black. He spoke excellent, crisp English and dressed smartly in the same khaki uniform that the First Mate was fond of wearing.

He had a strong military bearing and spoke softly as I scoured the horizon. When the sun began rising in the east; it cast a soft iridescent glow across the swells making the ocean appear as though it were filled with semi-precious jewels.

It didn't take long before the sun began to break over the horizon and flooded the wheelhouse with brilliant hues of gold and white.

At six in the morning; the Bosun's mate sent Arturo up to relieve me and I went down to the crew mess to eat breakfast. After eggs and ham and a quick cup of coffee; I returned to the wheelhouse and finished out my watch.

When eight o'clock arrived; I was relieved by Frank again. The can was empty. He asked the heading and punctuated my departure with a spit in the can.

I walked back to the crew mess and surprised Miguel by asking him for a cup of coffee in Spanish. It sounded stupid and clumsy, but Miguel took the compliment, and brought me a cup of coffee with a big grin on his face.

He rattled off a few comments in Spanish; I nodded smiling while not even beginning to comprehend what he was saying; and watched him as he returned to his morning dishes.

Hanz came into the galley; looked at me briefly; and then disappeared in the officer's mess. I had eight hours to kill. Andre hadn't been relieved yet so I waited in the crew's mess until he came in.

He was covered in the same filth as the night before.

I waited for him to shower and grab a cup of coffee and then we both headed up to the afterdeck.

Andre spoke first.

"I guess the cook is a little upset."

"Que?" I was practicing. I looked at him inquisitively. "What bug climbed up his stilted German ass?"

"The man the Captain brought on board and hired as Assistant Cook yesterday was supposed to work in the galley. Apparently he never showed up for work this morning. They knocked on his cabin door but he just ignored whoever they sent to wake him."

"Hanz is going to let him sleep it off and wake him up in time for him to help with lunch."

"The cook; how shall I say it? Es muy furioso! He is very angry."

I hadn't met the assistant cook yet. I saw him serving lunch and then again at the evening meal for the officers the day we left port. I didn't even know his name.

Conversation passed slowly between us. I was falling all over the Spanish language. When Andre's coffee cup was empty; I fetched two fresh ones from the galley and returned to my place on the afterdeck

I let Andre wander on about his days working on the cruise ships. I told him about my short excursion onto Dodge Island and my experience with the Customs Officers.

Cruise ships were a lot better place to work than pig boats such as these. Or so he led me to believe.

He'd work on them again someday. But he would stay away from New Jersey blonds too. Too much hassle, he said.

Miguel came through the hatch out onto the afterdeck wearing his apron. He was carrying a cup of coffee and a lit cigarette as he walked to the rail in front of us.

His hands were wrinkled from the dishwater. He could hold a burning coal from a cigarette between his fingers and never even feel it. He didn't say much. He just looked down at the propeller wash and drank his coffee; smoking his cigarette; watching the waves roll and fold.

Then he yelled excitedly; startling Andre and I. "Alli'!" "There! Over there!"

We looked and could see a pod of twelve.. maybe fifteen dolphins approaching the ship from the north. They surfaced several hundred yards off the starboard stern; watching us.

The dolphins moved in closer to us; watching; playing briefly; keeping effortless pace with the ship. And then like torpedoes they rocketed forward and left us plodding along in their seamless passage.

Their speed amazed me. They had to be doing forty, maybe fifty miles an hour when they passed us.

It opened up a new conversation for us.

Andre tried to explain some of the myths which surrounded the dolphin; and their less intelligent cousin; the porpoise. It wasn't long before I learned something new about Andre.

He launched into a fascinating recitation of the Rhyme of the Ancient Mariner. It took him almost a full hour to complete. I just sat there laughing in childish amazement. Miguel chain smoked away; listening; but not understanding and then politely excusing himself to return to the galley when Andre was finished.

"Andre. That was amazing! How long did it take you to memorize that?" I asked.

He looked over the rail and into the wash and said softly; "Years. My life. It has taken my life to memorize it."

It was a few minutes after Miguel left that Hanz reappeared on the afterdeck. He did not look happy. It was eleven in the morning.

Andre didn't take any crap from anyone. Hanz wasn't any exception. They had butted heads before. Andre and Hanz briefly exchanged words in Spanish. Hanz left fuming. After he left the afterdeck, Andre explained.

Hanz was still looking for the assistant the Captain had hired yesterday. The man's cabin was locked and no one answered the repeated knocks at the door. Hanz was furious by now. He assumed the man would be on the afterdeck. When he discovered that we were alone out here; it just infuriated him even more.

Hanz loved power; but he didn't have any. He was just a cook.

Hanz asked Andre if he had seen the assistant cook. Andre had sarcastically replied that it wasn't his turn to watch him.

Hanz had left in a fury to ask Riley. Riley was a drunk and it looked like the man the Captain had hired might be one as well. The ship was short one engineer. If Riley had hooked up with the assistant cook and drank the night away; there was a good chance the man would be sleeping in Riley's cabin.

Hanz had walked away muttering that the "captain would hear about this."

"The drunken fools. This was no way to run a ship."

"Oh. The Captain will hear of it. To be sure. Hanz is a whining, mean-spirited, friendless, hate-filled man who lived to make other people miserable." Andre said. "To be sure, the Captain will hear of it."

I didn't like Hanz. Nobody seemed to like him. They just seemed to tolerate him. No one messed with the cook though. He'd poison your food. Everybody just steered clear of him.

A big ship is still a very small place.

Like Andre had said. It is extremely difficult to get lost on a ship. It is extremely difficult to hide on a ship.

After Riley was rudely interrupted from his slumber and it was discovered that the assistant cook was not in his cabin; the search narrowed.

Riley had a few choice words for the cook.

The man had to be in his cabin or overboard.

When lunch came and went; the order was given to fetch the master key from the Captain.

When Hanz opened the cabin; his color changed from an angry red to a colorless white.

A sweet stench rolled out of the cabin like an invisible cloud; flooding the airless passageways with a nauseating, gagging foulness.

So quick and so surprising was it that it caused several of the spectators who had gathered to listen to Hanz give his dressing down to the new man to immediately vomit in the passageway.

They couldn't get topside quick enough.

When Hanz opened that door; the grim face and overpowering smell of death greeted him in the warm oven of a tropical day. This was no pie baking in an oven.

He'd been drinking alright.

By the looks of it; he'd been too drunk to lean over the rail to throw up in the night.

Instead; he had just drowned in his own vomit.

The body had begun to bloat in the tropical heat.

He had never bothered to open the porthole in his cabin.

Dinner would be sandwiches tonight. Hanz would be sick for a while.

Chapter Twelve

Davitch heard it first. Being younger; his senses are keener. He heard the ping over 200 miles away. Ebron did not hear it. A full day passed. Then we all heard it.

We have learned to avoid these machines of war, these machines of destruction. Their sonar are a peril to us. They deafen us. We turned south to avoid them. We avoid them at all cost. They kill many of us.

Our turn took us into the currents that would lead into the Appa Sea. It was a fortuitous event. The storm had left us on the fifth day and Davitch basked in a new found warmth; laying and rolling in the warm of the sun upon the ocean swells.

He was no longer a foundling. He had found his dolphin.

Tesla had taught him well. She was betrothed to him.

He was now beginning to learn things he had only begun to imagine possible. He was a teacher. He would teach us.

This would be his destiny. I was beginning to understand it. He had come to us to teach us. We loved him. He was so innocent. He was a child.

Ours is not like yours. We learn as we may. We do not judge. You judge everything. Everything in your world is judged. We judge nothing. Davitch was a child in our world. We loved him in a way you never could. We loved him in a way you never did.

It is your loss.

We do not seek to advance our grasp of technology because we know what you do not.

We seek instead to deepen the grasp of the mind that is given us in the Great Ocean. Davitch was new to ours.

Davitch is special. He understood this. He overcame his fear in the wildness of that summer storm. The ocean is nothing to fear. Life is nothing to fear.

Man, on the other; is something to fear. He fears you. Tell us why.

The sonar reached him; but not us; and made him circle Tesla for a day until she heard it. It told us we were well to listen. He is special.

"Yes. How is that you can detect it when I cannot?" She wondered aloud to all of us.

It was a question that made us all wonder. Who is this man-child among us?

His brain was awakening.

Ours had fallen to sleep.

We had reached a point after several moons; a place you call the Island of Birds. Davitch says it is Canaries. The islands of Canaries.

It is not the name we knew them as.

We are familiar with them. They are the peaks of mountains. They are not islands. It is close to the place of Sallon's birthing. It is a place of warm water.

We had crossed the place of peril without incident.

We would encounter fishermen of kindness here. We were a revered species here. There would be no nets or baited wires. There would be no rifle shots or harpoons. We would find welcome in these waters.

We rested for a week and fed on the fishes that mill about in these waters. Most of them are a tiny fish that are sweet and easy to catch.

Sardines.

Davitch calls them Sardines.

They are very good. Like a candy, he says.

Then we hovered and took the current along the coast. It was warm. The coasts were deserted. They were barren of life except for dunes and the occasional fishing boat.

The men here are black. They waved at our passing.

A few who waved begged us to fill their nets. We could see by their gestures their great poverty and hunger.

So we did. We filled their nets.

The five of us.

We went deep and used our skills to herd and chase the fish into their nets.

We filled the nets of those fishermen to overflowing. And then we leapt in a happy farewell. We laughed and snickered as we moved north along the coast. Eat well.

May they eat well.

We certainly did.

By this time Davitch did not need Tesla's pity. She had taught him to listen as she drove fish directly to him. He was growing. He was growing stronger by the day.

We watched as he and Tesla would test each other in their leaps.

Tesla always leapt a little higher.

But he was growing.

So was she. There was a young one inside her; growing. Her belly was beginning to distend. Davitch would roll underneath her and click and whistle to his unborn son.

They would make love in the morning and afternoon and evening.

He was insatiable. He was in love.

He had forgotten completely the world he had left behind.

When we reached the great rock we could taste the waters of the Appa Sea. We were not far. Another seven suns and we would see the first of the great ruins. Another seven suns and the understanding of this man-child would change again.

It would not be possible to take him to the deepest edge of our ruined continent; so deep had the chasm taken it. But we could show him the outer rings of our cities and their ruins. At the greatest height of our civilization here; they had spread across the planet.

Most evidence of them had been lost during the deluge.

We would cross into the Appa Sea through the straights.

It would lead to the lost city of the ancients. It would lead to the place where the greatest crimes had been committed. It would lead to the place where the greatest loss of our people had taken place.

We found others of our kind in the passing of the second sun after crossing through the narrow passage that opened into the Appa Sea.

The Delphi Pod were amazed to see us. They were amazed that we had traveled across the great sea in search of the old places.

They were stunned that we had brought a man-child with us.

There would be great discussion over what this event meant for the world. In our history; to our knowledge; it had never happened before.

There had been times when those of us wished to end their existence as dolphin and returned to land to live out their lives as human beings.

They were never heard from again. No one knew what happened to them.

Some speculated that they simply died of loneliness. Others speculated that they simply grew weary of life on this planet and returned to their Source; they simply went home again; never to return here.

But it was all speculation.

No dolphin descended from the Deluge had ever given up his life to hand it to a man; much less a child of a man. It was unheard of.

We spent several moons with the Delphi communicating and taking measure of their world.

It was not much different from ours.

Many dolphins had fled from the northern seas into the Appa. There seemed to be a migration of some kind occurring.

The young born in the northern waters were quickly dying after birth. The older dolphins were dying as well from illnesses that the intersects could not heal. Some of the older of the Delphi Pod suspected pollution of a man-made order. But the pollution had an invisible; tasteless nature to it.

Many from the north had come to the Appa Sea to die.

By the time the dolphins realized they were ill; it was to late to reverse the damage that had been done.

Most of it occurred on a cellular level suggesting that the pollution was radioactive in nature. The inland waters north of the Appa Sea were poisoned; dying, and would soon be dead.

The Delphi had learned as well that the thermohaline was changing. They were in constant deliberation about the meaning of this. The melting of the polar ice caps meant great consequences for the planet.

Already the Appa Sea was beginning to feel the effects of this. There were wild, unpredictable storms and long periods of drought and flood. The earth was awakening.

The intersects were beginning to show signs of fluctuation. We had seen this fluctuation before. But when before we did not know what it meant, now we had an idea.

The Delphi were trying to interpret those signs. They could mean anything. Or they could mean one thing. We had our own thoughts.

They asked us what we saw in our world. They wanted to know what the man-child saw in his.

We knew the damage that was being done by man.

We had watched our food sources dwindle over time as man became so efficient at harvesting the ocean that there was little left of the species that he took for them to reproduce. Man ranged further and further in search of fish. There was little left for us.

Soon he would return to his harbors empty handed

When this happened. We would begin to slowly starve ourselves.

We told the Delphi that the great coral reefs of the Sargasso Sea were dying. Human expansion on land had poured vast amounts of nitrogen and other poisons into the ocean creating huge blooms of algae which sucked the oxygen from the waters; killing even more life.

The ocean bottoms were littered with the cast off refuse of the human race.

The ocean had become one large dumping ground for all manner of poisons and human waste.

They had met by sheer accident several years earlier; a roving Penier; a rogue dolphin; who had traveled with the white ones as far into the northern reach as far as he could go. He had told us of hundreds of huge rusting ships loaded with thousands upon thousands of rusting barrels that were being sunk to the bottom of the ocean one by one. Sunk one by one on top of another.

They were loaded with the same poison that has killed the inland waters north of the Appa Sea. "There is a glowing mountain of this poison laying on the bottom of our home." he had said. "To travel near it is to invite a lingering death."

He fled south once he realized that his life was in peril from the leaking poisons on those ships. It will not be long before those poisons rust from their containers and make their way into the currents.

The Delphi had met a summer ago with pods of dolphins who had made their way west through the Islands of the Wili Water and then crossed the Sea of Storms. Davitch explained these were the oceans on the far side of the planet.

They had traveled quietly through the gates of what Davitch calls the Suez into the Appa Sea. From the Pacific and the Indian Oceans.

They told of a great disaster about to befall the inhabitants of those waters. It has been many years in coming; but man and animal alike are soon to harvest the consequences of the brutal savagery of man yet again. A generation is about to be remembered. The rusting giants of a forgotten conflict about to bleed their long submerged poisons into a pristine world.

They spoke of thousands of rusting hulks laying on the bottom of the sea slowly rusting away. The sunken remnants of a human war. Many of them have already begun to leak their untold destruction into the clean, clear water of the Islands around them. By their estimates; the problem is so vast; so huge; that there is no way to prevent the killing that comes.

One great storm will open many of the rusting hulls and end much; if not all of the life; that lives in that place.

So they fled here hoping for refuge.

But here is no different.

It is poisoned here as well.

We swim in poisoned water.

We do not know how long we have. Our food sources are diminishing by the day. Human efforts to expand and grow continue to add even more poison to the waters in which we live.

We do not know how much longer we have before we must flee ourselves.

Show the man-child the ruins of our ancient world, and then we will ask him the nature of his.

It was then that we took Davitch to the first intersect. We could feel it before we saw it. It pulsed through us as though it were alive. In many ways it is.

Humans can barely feel these centers of power. They are scattered about the face of the planet like fountains of water which spring up from the depths of the universe.

They have but one purpose to us now.

We come here to heal our wounds and our sicknesses. We come here to purify our hearts and our minds. We come here to beg forgiveness for our sins and seek redemption for our crimes. We come here to remind ourselves of what it was we have lost and what it is we serve in that loss.

The first intersect lies in 1300 feet of water now. The citadel has fallen; but the light from it still shines like a tiny beacon in the darkest of nights. The temples surrounding it have fallen into unrecognizable ruin. Made from the purest marble; they were shaken to the ground in broken shattered pieces when the shift occurred.

The roads that we built were cut from granite block and can be seen from space to this day leading out like spokes on a wheel away from the capital of our great civilization.

At one time; we thought we were the center of the universe.

We were mistaken.

Our harbors were the envy of all the world.

"Tell me what you see, Davitch?"

"I see a world that lived before ours and somehow perished long before ours ever thought of being."

"Yes."

"Swim into the light."

I watched as Davitch swam towards the ruins of the citadel. As he drew closer; I could see the gold of Sallon's rings begin to resonate inside him. I knew Davitch could feel it. I knew he could see things now that I would have taken many months to explain in words to him.

He stopped in the shimmering and hovered; barely moving; as though he was waiting for something to tell him it was time to go. Many things were happening to him in the light.

He was learning about us.

He was learning how the Deluge came to happen.

He was learning how we came to find this planet and colonize it.

He was learning how the intersect would use him to bring about the shift.

I did not believe he could hold his breath that long. I was almost ready to surface without him when he turned, came to me, and said simply; "I understand."

"It is time to go."

We rocketed to the surface and leapt from the water in unison taking a full breath of fresh air for the first time in many, many moments.

The Delphi were waiting for us.

Actually; they were waiting for Davitch.

"What did you learn in the intersect, Davitch?"

It was Eden's voice asking me; but I could hear the voices of the Delphi Pod adding to hers. They were all clamoring to hear what the intersect had shared or given.

"It is coming. The shift is coming. They are coming." said Davitch quietly.

The Delphi grew silent.

Eden spoke softly to Davitch.

"Davitch...how do you feel? Are you feeling differently?"

"No. Eden. I am fine. I am at peace. There is no stopping it. The planet is tired. It is tired of being abused. It is tired of being abused by creatures that it loves. It is awakening once more. How did Tesla put it? It is walking to the waterhole."

"It is not thirsty. It has something else in mind."

"There is something else. Your people are returning. They are already here. Mankind has caught glimpses of them; but for the most part; mankind does not know that they are coming. Some people know; but they are hiding it."

"Your people have returned. They have come in anticipation of the shift."

The intersect had done something to him. The intersect had reached into his mind and opened up parts of it to Davitch. He was seeing the shift as it applied to symbols in his old world. He was seeing the shift as it applied to his new world; to our world.

"Tell me more; Davitch. Tell us more; if you can. If you will." Eden was almost begging.

"It was a mistake to bring me here, Eden." Davitch said slowly. "Though I can live in your world for as long as I choose; I must one day return to my own."

"It is there my destiny lies. Sallon has returned to the world of men as well. He will live out his days as a man. But he is to be a great teacher among them. I do not know how I know this. I only know that I do."

"The intersect has shown me a great many things about both our worlds. It has showed me the pain that the world is in." he continued softly.

"Does the Delphi wish to see what I have seen in the intersect?"

"Does it wish to hear what it can already feel in my mind?"

"The Delphi already know that what I have said is truth. You said it yourself, Eden; there can be no secrets among us."

"The only thing the intersect did not tell me was the day when the shift would occur. It only said that certain things must come to pass first."

"And even then it made itself clear to me that not all of those things were necessary for the shift to occur. It could happen today. It may happen tomorrow. No one may say for certain. It is entirely up to us. But there is no stopping it."

"I cannot shake the feeling that anything we do will stop it. It is as though the intersect has said to me that there is no purpose for trying to stop it. It is a natural evolution. We just haven't been alive here long enough to witness it time and again. We cannot see the pattern to it. So we assume we are to be punished in it; by it."

"That is not why."

"The elephant will survive."

"The elephant will not be allowed to perish."

"Those who feed off the host will not be allowed to kill it."

"Davitch, tell me of our people. We have not told you this. How is it that you know they are returning?"

"They returned once before in search of you after the Deluge. But your people had vanished from the face of the planet. They retrieved what visible reminders of your existence remained. They collected your ships and your technology from what was left of your civilization. They left a few hidden sanctuaries for the Keepers of your Way."

"Humanity had returned quickly to a primitive state so they left quietly. They left the great structures your people had constructed as monuments to your arrogance and vanity; and as warning to human-kind."

"They are not returning; Eden. They are already here."

"They are simply waiting for the shift to occur. It is to be that soon."

Davitch was in a trance-like state as he communicated these things. His mind had been opened to new depths in the intersect. He was lost in the complexities and overwhelming magnitude of them.

The Delphi were silent. They had surrounded us and were listening quietly as Davitch opened his mind of his experience in the intersect.

"Tell me Davitch; How many of my people have come?"

"Many. Yours' Eden; there are many thousands who have come."

"There are others also who have come from all of the civilizations to take part in the shift."

"There are others; too; who have come to try to prevent it. But they have not come with the interests of this planet at heart. They have come as looters come."

"So what is to become of us; Davitch? What is to become of Dolphin?"

"A third more of us will perish in the nets; by harpoon; by pollution; by poison; by hunger.

"A third more will choose to return to the world of men after the shift takes place. They will become as Sallon has become. They will become human once again. They will become what they were first intended to be. They will become teachers."

"The last third will depart this planet with those who have come to witness the shift. They are to be pioneers once again in a new world devoid of human-kind. They are to become seeds once more. They are to be planted in a new soil."

"Once the shift is upon this planet; death will resemble life in many ways. But the planet will not die. It will only change."

"The oceans of this planet are almost dead. They have reached a point where they can no longer sustain the life that depends on them. Man is solely responsible for this. He is the fly."

"The change in the thermohaline is almost complete. Soon it will fold. When this occurs; the human species will slowly begin to understand fully the magnitude of the havoc it has invited."

"There is so much, Eden. There is too much."

"I would like to go back now to the place where you found me."

"Yes, of course Davitch. But why."

"Because I would like our son birthed in those waters. I have decided upon the name I will give him. It is the name given to me in the intersect."

"What has been chosen as his name?" Eden asked gently.

"He will be called Juha."

"It means "First among the many.""

The Delphi pod begged us to remain with them. They had many more questions for Davitch. But I could tell there was something in his tone that was begging us to leave. We would spend one more night with the Delphi and leave on the sunrise through the straits.

We would follow the sun west to the peaks of the Minoan range and then head south west toward the Sargasso Sea through the triangle.

If what Davitch said was anywhere near the truth; and I had absolutely no reason to doubt him; we would see evidence of it in our crossing.

The Delphi were saddened to see us go.

It was almost as though they knew they would never see us again.

That much was true.

If the shift was as close as Davitch said the intersect suggested it was; there could be many things we would never see again.

Ebron took sides with Tesla and Davitch and began speaking with Davitch.

"You did not say much about the world of men to the Delphi. Was there a reason for that, Davitch?" Ebron asked quietly.

His reply was slow and deliberate. "I did not answer for their benefit, Ebron. I did not answer for mine. I did not ask to see what I saw. The intersect is a thing of great wonder and beauty. I realized when I first swam into the light how it could be used for great good. I saw too how it could be used for a great harm."

"How could your people do what they did?" Davitch asked angrily.

"How could they think that there would be no consequences to the things that they had done?"

"Your people offended nature. Your people offended the universe. Did they honestly believe the universe would allow those offenses to go unpunished? Did they believe the universe would allow that imbalance to endure?"

"I am struck first by the intelligence of your race and then I am breath taken by the sheer and utter stupidity of it!"

"Ebron. How did it happen?"

"We became human. How else can I say it? We were overtaken by the nature of this world, Davitch. We had so much power at our command. We had so much technology at our fingertips. There was no greater authority to hold us back. So we did as we chose."

"This is the great lesson we learned in the great mistake that we made, Davitch."

"We learned that technology alone does not give you power. We learned that technology alone does not have a goodness to it or an evil to it. It is the hands that hold that technology that makes it good or evil."

"We learned many things in our first days after the Deluge. There is indeed a difference between having the right and having the power. We had the power. We did not have the right. Our civilization had been crushed in one day by the universe for the crimes we had committed. The elephant did indeed take many of us in his roll."

"We learned that a technology that has lost it's purpose in the Light is doomed to fumble in the dark. We learned that a technology that would rather play in the darkness; will not see its own ugliness when the Light finally does indeed come to dispel it once again."

"We had become shadows of ourselves. We pretended to be gods; but in fact; we had become slaves to ourselves. We had become slaves to greed and lust. The majority of our medical and scientific efforts were spent in perfecting and achieving a perfect sexual experience, a longing to lust. Our science devoted itself to sustaining our physical bodies and enhancing the achievement of our sexuality, satisfying our cravings, in whatever form they took.."

"Our human slaves became our specimens. We conducted many inhumane experiments on them that offended nature."

"It is why we have chosen to live out our existence in this form on this planet. We are still a sexual creature. We are a tactile, sensitive animal. But we can do no more harm and can commit no more obscenity in this form. Do you understand?"

"Davitch. You of all of us know how weak the human species can be. We know the things you have suffered at their hands. Think of a race that had no moral compass, no religious taboos. Then wonder at what depravation our species was once capable of?"

"We deserved our punishment. We are a lesson your species would do well to learn from. But it has become more than that."

"We did not poison this planet and our souls as your species has done. We only poisoned ourselves. We only poisoned our own souls. They no more belonged to us than the planet did. That was part of our undoing as well."

"We became an affront to nature. In our ego; our arrogance; our depravity; we became an ugliness; a pain that threatened the existence of the universe itself. So the elephant walked to the watering hole and rolled."

"Those of us who survived; fled. We did so promising never to take a human form again until we had learned what it was to give instead of what it had become to take. We have spent many centuries seeking atonement for our transgressions. We had come as teachers to this place. Instead we became tyrants and torturers. It is a shame we will never allow ourselves to forget."

The sun rose upon the Delphi pod. They followed us to the straits and bid us farewell.

"What third are we among?" they seemed to be saying as we left them silently as keepers of the old places of the Appa Sea.

Chapter Thirteen

"I am disposable. I am temporary. I am the target. I am abused."
"I will become temporary. I will be your target. I am a bruise."

When I left the bus station; I knew deep down I was leaving for good. Who wants to run away to live in a bus station? I knew I had to go. I had to go somewhere. I wasn't paying rent and I had watched them shuffle some of the winos out the door during the night. I was just a better clientele.

I just didn't know where I was going. I crossed the bus station off the list. I was done here too. I had nothing to carry so it didn't matter if I walked a hundred miles.

I suppose I was in some kind of daze. The streets were just starting to wake up. I hadn't slept. Who was I kidding?

I had absolutely no idea what I was going to do. I just believed everything would turn out alright. I know I was hurting badly; but I was also excited in a way to be free. I was free of the tyranny of the foster care system. I was free. I was lost. But I was free. And I was hungry.

I hated those people. I hated that system. I had almost killed myself to hurt them. Some logic, huh? I'll show you. I'll hurt me.

It was early morning and I was hungry and tired, angry; and more lonely than I had ever been before in my life.

I just started walking.

One foot in front of the other.

I am amazed in this moment at how much I came to love some of the people I was about to meet. I will try to do them justice.

It was not all darkness.

Some of my memories are of great beauty.

To this day; I'm not sure how I ended up back there.

But all of a sudden I was standing in the same yard where the sewer tiles had been stacked. I was standing at the foot of a gangplank in front of a huge ship that had tied up during the night at a wharf in this yard.

Here I was standing in front of this big old rust bucket of a ship and I didn't even remember how the hell I got there.

A brown-skinned man in a khaki uniform was standing at the top of the gangplank trying to ask me what I wanted and all I could come up with was "huh?"

"Good going, kid. Take a little look around. Recognize this place? Yep, that's right. This is the wharf where your little green bag boarded a boat for parts unknown."

"Now talk to the nice man. He's asking you a question."

"I'm looking for a job. I'm looking for work."

That's how I introduced myself to a man I would come to know as William Eubanks; formerly of the Island of Roatan; and presently First Mate and gang boss on the 700 foot Motor Vessel Rita II.

"And why should I hire you, kid?" he asked gruffly.

Uh....because I'm really a great kid. I know lots of funny jokes...I...uh...I uh...I uh...

"Because I speak a little Spanish."

"Y donde aprendiste hablar espanol?" he asked.

I did it now. I slept though Spanish class in school. It was a joke.

I had to pick the only guy on the boat who was bilingual. He just asked me where I learned to speak Spanish.

"In High School." I lied.

"I learned how to speak Spanish in High School." All seven weeks of it.

Oh really? Well! That is impressive! Now you get to show him just how little you know. No. Stop...What I really meant to say was that... what I really meant to tell him was that I don't really speak it. I just had two years of it in Junior High School and I didn't really learn jack squat about it except how to swear in it because I was too busy getting high with the other stoners outside behind the bleachers.

Oh sure. I could conjugate a few verbs. One's like; I fuck. You fuck. Go fuck yourself. But that was the extent of it. I couldn't find my way to a bathroom in a Spanish Hacienda if I had a map in my hand. I was lying.

He knew it. But I was pretty sincere about it. He had to give me credit for that. I just wanted to work. Trabajo. Work. To work. Trabajar.

"Come aboard." he yelled.

I looked around. You mean me? On the boat? You want me to come aboard the boat? Up the gangplank? Yes sir! Right away, Sir! Here I come right now. I am walking up the gang plank, to talk to you about working on this fine, rusting piece of shit boat ship of yours right now this very minute yes SIR! About a job. Yes Sir!

Providence. It was the universe trying desperately to save me from myself.

Now. Remember. Sit up straight. Don't fidget or pick your nose or anything. And use lots and lots of Sirs. Yes sir. No sir. Three bags full, sir. Yes sir. And whatever you do. Lie. Lie like a rug or you'll be doing the Biscayne Boulevard shuffle by nightfall!

"You got it kid?"

"Yes SIR!"

Do or say whatever you have to; but get this job; whatever it is.

"What are you applying for anyway, kid? Just out of curiosity?"

"Yes Sir. That's right. I'm applying for the position of Captain. Oh.... That position is already taken..... I see.... Well..... Do you have anything else? Deck hand? Mess boy. Cabin boy? Anything? Anything at all?"

I was a mess. William Eubanks knew that from the minute he first laid eyes on me. He could see and probably smell that I was not having an easy time of it.

But I have these eyes. I have these gentle eyes. The kind I was once told that just beg for beatings. And Willy Eubanks took a long, hard, deep look into them.

He probably knew by the way I climbed the gangplank clutching both handrails that I didn't know squat about ships. This wasn't any rowboat I had climbed aboard.

The MV Rita or the Rita as we came to so fondly call her; was a rusting behemoth. It was an old ore boat that had been taken out of service in the freshwater of the Great Lakes and put to service in the very salty brine of the Atlantic ocean.

The only thing holding it together was rust. Huge plates of rust.

Chunks of rust, rusted to other huge chunks of rust. The deck moved and bubbled when you walked across it.

"This way boy."

"Wake up boy; this way!"

"Yes sir."

We headed off to the stern of the vessel and entered a hatch that took us down into the bowels of the ship. Everything was vibrating.

The whole ship seemed to be vibrating down here. I could hear a deep groaning hum coming from somewhere down below the deck. The passageways were hot and humid and smelled of human sweat and dirty clothes.

"Well, this is a plus." I thought, "Nobody down here is going to notice that I haven't bathed in a while."

"In here. Sit down. I'll be right with you." Hey this guy means business and he isn't even wearing a gun. This must be where I get the job interview.

We were sitting in the officer's mess. The portholes were filthy and looked out on the waters of Biscayne Bay. You could almost see Miami River from here.

Willy Eubanks went to the galley door and called for two cups of coffee.

"You want something to eat kid? Have you had breakfast yet?"

Oh. Yeah. I had one of those continental breakfasts they serve the winos up at the Greyhound Bus Station.

"Uh yes..no sir..I mean I'd like something to eat; yes sir; and no sir; I haven't had any breakfast yet sir."

"How quickly hope springs in the human heart. I about fell out of my chair when he asked me if I wanted something to eat. You mean food, sir? To eat? Is there any other kind dummy? Uh no; thank you; but a waxed pear would be nice, thank you. Gee kid, maybe you should get down on your knees and kiss his ass."

"Got enough "Sirs" in there, do ya? You better hope you do because the odds are you ain't going to be around long if this little venture doesn't pan out."

I knew my life was riding on a razor's edge that morning. I prayed a silent prayer that I would be hired. Anything. I will do anything. Just hire me. I will work for food.

The First Mate returned with two steaming mugs of black coffee from the galley.

"You'll have to drink it black. The ship's agent should be by this morning with fresh groceries. We've been out of fresh milk and bread and a bunch of other things for a few days now. We just got in last night."

The First Mate was half black; half Indian. He was Mulatto. He spoke English with a throaty Spanish accent and mixed his statements with a lot of grunts to emphasize that he heard you or wanted you to think he heard you.

He was clean shaven. In his late fifties maybe. He kind of reminded me of the Skipper on Gilligan's Island the way he wore the Khaki hat of his. He had a bit of a pot belly and walked stiffly; like maybe he had hurt his back at one time.

You could almost call it a saunter. He sauntered across the blazing deck. It kind of fit him.

I just sat there kind of respectful; holding the coffee with both hands; waiting for him to take a drink of his. He set his cup down and sat down across the table.

"The pay is $140.00 a month. We pay a dollar an hour for overtime. That includes your room and board. I need to see some identification for the ship's log.

I reached for my wallet and the phony I.D. card.

He looked at it and asked "Is this all you have?"

"Yes sir. Its all I have."

"It'll do."

"Well, you sit here and eat breakfast. The cook will show you to your berth after you finish. I'll send the Bosun's mate down to get you and you can start work this morning. After work you can go and get your things, wherever they are."

Thank you. Thank you. Thank you. Ask me no questions and I'll tell you no lies. Something crossed between us. He didn't want anything from me. Kindness. It has no name. It has no face. It just appears in the strangest of places.

As he got up; he looked at me a second time for a minute and looked me dead straight in the eyes and said "And kid; do me one favor will ya?"

At that point I would have killed for him. I was that hungry and that grateful

"Yes sir; whatever you need; sir."

"Take a shower. This place smells bad enough without adding to it. The cook will show you where the head is."

"Uh yes sir; you bet sir."

"And one other thing kid."

"Sir?"

"Don't make me regret doing what I just did."

I looked down at the table and then looked up at him with my eyes shining.

"I'll try not to sir. I promise."

"You do that."

He walked out the way he had come.

The cook brought me my breakfast in the officers mess.

He set my plate down, looked me over; stuck out his hand and said; "I am Hanz. I am the cook."

He was the cook alright.

He had brought a big steaming plate of scrambled eggs, bacon, and potatoes. The toast was conspicuously absent; but I was starved and couldn't have cared less. I was genuinely thankful for the life that had just opened like a blossom before me.

Hanz took a seat across from me and crossed one leg over the other and leaned his chin on his hand like he was observing a piece of art.

"So. You are an American. Yes?

"Yes."

"You are going to work on this boat. Yes?"

"Yes."

"What? You don't have anything better to do with your life than to work on this boat. No?"

"Yes..I mean no."

"I am German."

"From Germany. Yes?"

"Yes."

Only I could tell by his tone that he hadn't liked the way I had said it. I think he thought I was making fun of him because he frowned; got up; and said; "Bring your dishes to the galley when you are done."

I had one sarcastic mouth back then. One that got me in a lot of trouble at times. A bad attitude didn't help matters much either.

Hanz was German alright.

He was a good cook though.

I guess it doesn't matter what language you scramble eggs in.

It didn't take me long to finish.

I got up and walked to the Galley.

A tall lanky Spanish kid walked up to me and took my dishes from me. I stood there looking into the galley at the sinks and stoves; the walkin coolers, the food preparation table.

We used to kill rats in the galley at night by trapping them under the stoves.

Hanz was waiting for me. He led me down an opposite passageway until we came to a row of cabins. We entered one that had three berths in it. The berths had wooden rails on them. They looked like oversized cribs in a way. One berth was set alone against a bulkhead and two were stacked upon each other like bunk beds on a far wall. Bunk berths. Cool.

"This is your berth." he said, pointing to the upper berth. "Your clothes go in this drawer here and the head is outside the door on the right."

All in all, it wasn't so bad. Once you got used to the smell it really wasn't bad. Hell; it was a place to sleep. I had already eaten. Things were looking up. It was hotter than the hubs of hell; but I wasn't about to start complaining now.

Hanz returned a few minutes later and handed me some towels and linen and a woolen surplus navy blanket. He left without saying a word.

I stripped and wrapped a towel around me and walked the few feet to the head. The place stank of mildew and urine but the water was fresh and cool. I used the slivers of soap that were growing in the shower stall to wash with; clumping three or four of them together to make a mini-bar that didn't last long but seemed to do the job.

I was clean for the first time in over a week and I felt one hundred percent better. Gone was the dust of the yard and the many hundreds of miles of the trip south. Gone was the grime of the bus station and the sweat of the endless walk around Miami.

I dressed in my jeans and returned to the head with my socks and t-shirt. I washed them and wrung them out as best I could. The shirt would dry in no time. The socks would take a little longer.

I was making my bunk when the Bosun's mate came in. It was almost eight in the morning. He was from Honduras too and didn't speak a lick of English. He shook hands with me and I immediately liked him. He pointed to his eye and then at me.

Oh. You want me to get something out of your eye? No. That's not it. Let's see. I have beautiful eyes? No. That's not it either. Oh. I get it. You want me, right, to watch you, right? Yep. Bingo. Ok boss. You got it.

We headed up the ladder which opened onto the deck above the galley. The sun was really warming things up. Miami was really a nice place to be. It was colder than hell where I had just come from. My t-shirt was dry in about thirty seconds.

There were several trucks pulling into the area where the ship was tied up. A car wheeled around to the base of the gangplank and a man in his early forties got out. Willy met him at the top of the gangplank and they shook hands like old friends. They both looked over at the Bosun's Mate.

Willy shouted in Spanish and the Bosun's mate tugged my sleeve and we both headed over to the gangplank. It was time to earn my breakfast.

Four hours and about five hundred boxes of food later we had finished. I watched and listened the whole morning and worked like a dog. I never paused for a minute. I wasn't going to give anybody any reason for firing me. I wanted to be here for lunch and dinner. And maybe breakfast as well.

I just kept carrying box after box of food off the trucks up the gangplank; down into the galley; into the walk in coolers; and back up and down again; over and over and over. I'd never seen so much food in one place except maybe in a grocery store.

I had hope. I felt an enormous hope. If I can only make it here for a while. Make some money. Make some friends. Learn as much as I could. I would keep my smart mouth shut and do whatever was asked of me. I wasn't going back to the bus station. I wasn't going back.

I didn't know what Miami was about. I didn't know what anything was about. I was in awe of just about everything. I had been shuffled around in foster homes. I had even been shuffled to Texas to live for a year. I was tired of being shuffled. But to be on my own?

Miami was beautiful in a way.

The city looked so pretty with the palm trees and white coral.

I was just fifteen. I had just turned fifteen. I was doing it. I was going to be ok. I would be ok if I just kept my ass out of trouble.

Everything I had touched up to that point in my life had turned to shit. My life so far was one big bruise after another. I was constantly looking for ways to numb the pain I was in. I was always alone.

Maybe this would be different.

I was just a kid still. I wasn't even shaving yet, but I knew more about the kinks and the kooks than most writers for Hustler magazine did.

I was lost even then and I had absolutely no idea where we were headed or what I was doing. All I was interested in the moment was my next meal; where it was coming from; and where I was going to be sleeping that night. I had those bases covered. I would let the anxieties of tomorrow wait until they got here. For today; I had enough.

It was a crap shoot of cosmic proportion. I had rolled the dice this morning and come up sevens. I'll take them.

God knows I could use them.

But I was on my own and from this point on I would decide what was going to happen to me.

During the course of that first day, I made eye contact with other members of the crew during the loading and nodded a brief hello; but I didn't say much more than that.

When we broke for lunch, I was drenched in sweat. There is no worker like the hungry and the scared. The Bosun's Mate looked at me; put his hand to his mouth; and made a motion like he was putting food in it. I get you. It's time to eat. Lunch? Right? Comida? Si? Si! Comida!

At least I could remember a few words from my naps in Spanish class.

We went down into the cabin area and washed up for lunch. One hour. Rice and beans and stewed chicken. Fresh milk. Coffee.

Room and Board. One hundred and forty dollars a month. It was November 22nd. Not that it mattered but it was just a day I remembered. Kennedy had been assassinated on that day. My younger brother's birthday would be tomorrow. I felt a pang of sorrow thinking it.

He would be twelve...thirteen? I would have to do the math later.

Sometimes the loneliness was like a wave. It would wash over me and you could tell when it happened. I hardly ever smiled unless I knew someone was looking at me. I didn't dwell on it very long. I just let it go until the wave came and washed over me again. My loneliness. It was all I had at times.

After the loading was finished; we spent the rest of the day cleaning a stinking putrid hold that looked like a huge underground metal box. The ladder that led down into the hold was solid and welded into the bulkhead.

If you fell from that thing while you were climbing down; you were going to get hurt. There wouldn't be any scrapes or bruises in that fall. You would break major bones into little tiny splinters in that plummet.

Or worse. You'd be dead.

I met Arturo and Frank in the hold that afternoon. Both of them were from Honduras. It was beginning to seem like everybody on the ship was mostly from Honduras. Frank was from the mainland. Willy and Arturo were from the Island of Roatan. Both Frank and Arturo spoke passable English.

And both of them were blacker than coal.

The rest of the deck gang had pulled the hatch covers off during the morning while we had brought the groceries aboard. The Bosun's mate lowered five gallon pails down into the hold by rope and we swept and shoveled huge chunks of rusted steel into the pail and watched them disappear into the light above our heads.

When we called it quits at the end of the evening; we were covered in little tiny flakes of rust and dirt. I was drenched in sweat and starting to smell like a locker room again.

I was supposed to go get my stuff; wherever it was and hustle on back to the ship. That was going to be easy. I'll just make a quick swim down to El Guatemala or wherever real quick. I'll be back in say; oh, maybe a month or so.

No chance. I'm not getting off this boat. I'm not leaving. I'll stall.

There was no way I was leaving to go pretend to get something I knew didn't exist. Not only was it stupid; it was just plain stupid.

"Good thinking, kid. You need to make a friend and maybe borrow something. Maybe you could get an advance on that big fat check you have coming at the end of the month and go buy yourself some new duds at Lord & Bentleys or somewhere. Sure. Sure you can."

So how much do you think you earned today, kid? Can you do the math?

How much do you think you have coming? Four, maybe five bucks? That will go a long way. Think kid. Think. Think. Think. Just follow the crowd, listen; and play it by ear.

I ran the same routine as I did after breakfast. I washed up for dinner; ate; and then hit the shower. I washed my shirt again in the sink and then dawdled; hoping nobody noticed I was dragging ass. They didn't. There were a few curious looks but nobody said anything to me about my not leaving the ship.

The workday was over for me.

I wandered up to the afterdeck after my shower. I was trying to explore the ship without being conspicuous. The back deck had a few chairs on it and it looked like a good place to kill a few minutes and assess the events of the day and my next move.

"Hola. Que' esta passando?"

"Huh?"

"Oh. You are the American Willy brought on board this morning. I was asking how you are doing?"

"I was just looking at the skyline." I mumbled.

He got up and walked over to the rail where I was standing and stuck his hand out. "My name is Andre. I am from Nicaragua."

He pumped my hand a couple of times; dropped it; looked at the skyline and said, "Yes it is quite beautiful isn't it?"

I just kept looking out at it.

He had that right.

Miami has a strange allure. At night it looked like a crown set with all manner of rubies and emeralds and jewels. The flickering greens and reds and blues were like semi-precious stones lighting up the darkness.

The cruise ships across the bay glowed white in the backdrop of the starlit sky. It was just last night I was there.

Andre saw me looking toward Dodge Island and said "I used to work on the Empress. Would you like something to drink?

He was drinking straight from a quart bottle of Smirnoff Vodka and he handed it toward me.

It wasn't like I had never had a drink before. Might as well have a drink.

Hell. I had earned one given the events of the past week. I could use a drink.

"Sure. Thanks Andre."

"Cigarette?"

"Sure. Thanks again."

Andre was the first friend I made.

I suppose you could count Willy. But he was the First Mate. There would be no fraternization between officers and crew. We pulled up chairs and sat. I remember spending the next few hours with Andre sharing what truth I felt comfortable sharing with him. The vodka made it easier.

Soon the subject of my clothes came up. I didn't have any.

Andre wasn't surprised. He just smiled this sly smile that I would come to love.

Miami was full of people who were running somewhere from something. It was full of ships that were full of men who were all running from something. Many of them were running hard and traveling light. It didn't matter.

After the bottle was half empty, Andre smiled that sly grin of his and said, "Clothes? You need clothes, kid? I'll show you clothes."

He laughed and said "Follow me."

We half walked, half stumbled down into the engine room where Andre led me to a huge bin filled with rags.

"And what size do you wear, Sir? He shouted over the roar of the generators.

That's how I ended up with my new wardrobe. Andre worked as a wiper in the engine room and from that day on I had all the clothes I could wear.

The night ended with an empty bottle of Smirnoff and Andre pouring me into my berth. I was so drunk I didn't care that I was alone. I had made a friend. It was a beginning. It was enough.

Andre would teach me; show me the ropes; lend me things if I asked. I was sure of that. I had a bed to sleep in. I had eaten three meals today. It was enough. We were sailing the next day at noon.

I didn't even know where we were headed and I didn't care.

Morning came with the sound of men stirring about. Coughing. Farting. The Bosun's Mate gently shook me awake. "Levantate'" he said.

I swung my feet over the wooden rail looking for the floor, lost my balance and fell out of my bunk. Yeah, that's right kid. You got the top bunk. Or don't you remember? Nah. Why should you? You were half-dead drunk when Andre rolled you in there.

I started for the head and caught sight of Andre at the end of the passageway standing in a towel talking to Riley, the Chief Engineer. Andre had shaving cream on his face and was holding a toilet kit in his hand. He looked in my direction and smiled and shouted, "Eh, so we are alive this morning? We have a big day today. We sail at noon."

Andre finished his conversation with Riley and headed down the passageway toward me.

"Here. You will need these. You can pay me back later."

The kit had soap; a package of disposable razors, a toothbrush; and a tube of Spanish toothpaste in it. It was all coming back to me now.

"Leaving? Where are we going?"

"We go to the Yucatan for salt." Andre said. "Quick. Get cleaned up and meet me in the crew mess. We will talk over breakfast."

With that he turned and headed back down the passageway.

"Gees kid, one minute you're crying like a baby outside the Greyhound Bus station. The next minute you're on a ship headed for Mexico. When things happen for you; they happen real quick like; huh?"

Yeah. They sure do. No shit. Mexico. I'll be dipped. I was saved. I actually felt like things just might work out. It was a good start.

Andre was already in the crew mess. He had saved me a seat beside him at the table and poured me a cup of coffee. Other members of the crew were already there as well. Arturo was at the end of the table with Frank and there were a couple of men I hadn't met yet.

An older man came to the half door and asked me if I was going to eat breakfast.

"Yes sir. I'll have whatever you got. Thank you."

Andre smiled. "I trust you slept well? You were feeling pretty good when you hit the rack."

"More like passed out. I was tired and the vodka made it even worse."

"I see you went and got your things, eh?"

I picked up on his tone immediately. I replied loud enough for anybody who was interested in hearing. "Yeah. I didn't have much to go and get." And that was the end of that.

No one would ever know it was rags I was wearing. It was better clothing than some of the stuff I had as a foster child.

We ate our breakfast and went up on deck where the Bosun's mate was waiting. It was going to be another beautiful day in Miami. I can understand why people love Miami; why they love Florida. The weather is beautiful most of the time.

That's one of the reasons I picked Florida when I ran. I figured if I was going to have to sleep in a park or under a bridge somewhere until I got situated; at least I wouldn't freeze to death.

It was snowing where I was when I left.

Two huge tanker trucks had pulled up in the yard. Riley was standing in the entrance to the engine room and yelling and pointing. There is little doubt in my mind that Riley had one of the foulest mouths I had ever heard. About every third word was an obscenity. It was comical to listen to.

Some of the things he suggested were anatomically impossible to do but that didn't stop him from suggesting it.

He finally threw up his hands; stormed down the gangplank; and snatched one of the nozzles out of one of the driver's hands. With a greatly exaggerated effort he slowly and comically inserted the nozzle into the ship's fuel tank fill.

Talk about making a guy feel stupid. Well, the guy was stupid. Or he was playing stupid.

The Bosun's mate grabbed me and we headed forward. Andre disappeared into the engine room.

We opened the forecastle hatch and walked into the stifling heat. It was cramped, musty and smelled of old rope, grease, and cement.

We spent the next three hours mixing concrete and packing the anchor chain runnels for the voyage. They were huge. You could slide your whole body down them. The anchor chain links were ten inches in diameter.

The way the Bosun's mate explained it to me in sign language was; now let me see if I can get it right; oh....yeah; The ship is moving along and comes to this really big wave and then whoosh! See! When the bow of the ship hits the wave, all this water comes rushing up the runnels, see? The water floods this tiny little room, see? It gets everything wet.

Not to mention of course that the water flows down the hatch that opens into the forward hold right here, see? That's a bad thing. See? Yeah. I could see where flooding the boat with water could be a problem.

Now how big were these waves again? Big huh. About as high as me?

No? Bigger? How much bigger? Yeah? No shit. Them's are big waves.

No kidding. Are we using enough concrete.? Shouldn't we use a little more just to be on the safe side?

We took up the slack in the anchor chain and tied it to a niggerhead inside the forecastle with a two inch line. It wasn't going anywhere; no matter how big those wave got. When we were done the Bosun's mate pointed at his eye and gestured for me to follow him.

The Miami sun was blazing now. Willy was on the deck above the forecastle shouting orders in Spanish to the men and Riley was in the mid ship crane between the two holds. They had a cable attached to the gangplank and were hoisting it over the wire rail.

A couple of men had lines on it and were guiding it down on the hatch cover over the aft hold.

By the looks of it; you'd think the ship was leaving or something.

"Put a hand on the lines! Willy bellowed.

The men stationed on the bow and stern lines slipped the three inch hawsers as men on shore let them drop into the water. The winches began to whine as they slowly pulled them in. The starboard winches began to whine as a tugboat tied on the Bayside of the ship slowly groaned as it powered up and edged the Rita toward Government Cut.

As soon as the Rita was headed east toward the Atlantic; the open sea; the tugboat cut loose and Willy shouted again.

"Make for the open sea! Stand to watch!" Then he disappeared into the bridge.

The bosun's mate smiled at me, tugged my sleeve, and pulled me toward the bow of the ship. He reached into his shirt and offered me a cigarette.

Enjoy the view, kid. This is it. Take a good look. You won't be seeing Miami again for a while.

The ship moved slowly up Government Cut; passing Dodge Island and a half a dozen cruise ships tied up there on the Starboard; and Chalk's Seaplanes on Watson Island on the Port. The Goodyear Blimp was anchored serenely in a field next to MacArthur Causeway and I could see faces in the cars as they watched us head out to sea.

"Hey look over here. Watch me! Can you do this?"

It took us about twenty minutes to pass the Coast Guard Station on the edge of Miami Beach and then Government Cut was behind us.

We were finally at sea and heading South. Miami was growing smaller.

It was time for lunch. I'd come back to the bow and watch the coastline disappear after I ate.

Chapter Fourteen

Davitch fell silent as we made our way across the Minoan range. The waters of this place were mostly deserted of human activity. Occasionally we would spot a commercial fishing vessel; but we stayed far away of them.

We had re-entered dangerous waters. There were deep and inhabited by fish much larger than ourselves.

We had once again become food.

Davitch was as confused as confused could be. We all sensed it. His recollections of his short life did not allow for the perspective that we have. We know that it takes many lives to understand the balance necessary to live in this world.

Earth is the jewel in the crown of heaven. To come here and live here is a gift that all souls wish for. Finding balance is not an easy thing to do among the many illusions that are found here. There are so many; and they are so tempting.

We all felt a bit of sorrow for him. We knew that he did not deserve the life we had designed for ourselves when we fled in the Deluge. We had grown accustomed to this existence over many centuries.

This was our existence now.

We knew; each of us; that he would one day return to the world of men.

We just did not know when.

He was innocent. His heart was pure. Every living creature has a spirit born from the fountain of life. Human beings have a soul. It is what makes them greater than the fly.

Davitch knew many things now that would forever change his understanding of the world. Regardless of whether or not he chose to remain in our world or return to his; his mind would never return to it's former understanding. He could not unlearn the things we had shown him.

He could not unlearn the things he had seen in the intersect.

We traveled for seven days in silence; following the sun across the sky; and played and slept in turns during the gentle nights that followed.

It was on the eighth night that Tesla was taken from us.

It was an accident.

We were all tired.

We had all fallen to sleep together.

Tesla's screams brought us immediately awake.

We counted three of the great whites upon her and a fourth moving in toward Ebron. And then a fifth. And then a Sixth. Then seven.

Davitch struck one of the whites that had attacked Tesla with such a fury that he killed it outright.

Tesla had no chance. She had been taken in her sleep and been ripped apart even as she died.

Our only choice was to flee.

We were outnumbered. We were tired. They were upon us.

We had no choice but to flee. Tesla was gone. There was no saving her.

Beautiful Tesla. Her unborn son. Both were gone.

Davitch. Where is Davitch?

He was blinded by his fury. He killed one more of the great whites before he fled. One of them opened a glancing wound near his left pectoral. The pain of the wound brought him back to our world.

"Davitch! You must flee! Follow us! Now! They cannot follow us! Or you will die! Please! Tesla is gone! Do not leave us too! Please, Davitch! Flee Now!"

Davitch turned and followed us. But not until he inflicted another furious blow on one of the smaller whites that had risen from the depths to feed on Tesla's corpse.

By the time he rejoined us his wound had ceased to bleed. We had left the great whites many miles behind us.

Davitch was in shock.

He was blind in his grief. We were all blind in our grief.

So this is to be our destiny.

To be lost one by one.

To lose one another one by one.

I am Keeper of Our Way. We said goodbye to Tesla by the Ritual that is Our Way.

In the recesses of my heart I wondered for a fleeting moment if this was not the Great Ocean's punishment for having crossed that barrier in the first. Was Tesla's man-child an abomination to the Universe?

I would never know.

Or was it just a tragic accident?

We had dropped our guard and lowered our defenses in waters we knew were dangerous and Tesla paid the price for our dereliction; my dereliction. We were tired and frightened and the world was a lonely; dangerous; hopeless place that was fast becoming more inhospitable by the day.

Tesla had joined the third who would not see the world of men. She had joined the third who would not pioneer another world. She had joined the third who would die before the shift.

What third did I belong to? Or Neva? Or Ebron?

What of Davitch? What third of dolphin did he belong to? What did he have to keep him in our world now?

We were nearing the warmer waters of the Sargasso. It would be a conversation that would bring great pain to the heart of this creature who loves us. He has been through so much.

To lose so much and now to lose Tesla.

I cannot bear this child's grief. How is it that he can begin to bear his own?

"Davitch?"

"Yes, Eden. I am with you."

"I am so sorry."

"It was not your fault, Eden. I knew when I left the intersect that one of us would be lost in the crossing. I was hoping it would be me. I was hoping I was wrong. I wondered. I said nothing. I should have said something. I am to blame."

"No. Davitch; there is a reason for everything. What will you do now?"

"You are loved among us. You are so loved among us. What does your heart tell you now?"

"I will stay with you, Eden, for a little while; and grieve for Tesla and Juha. I will not leave you to grieve for them alone. We will find peace in their loss. Then I must return to my world. You know it must be this way just as I know it must be so."

"But just as I must leave, Eden; I would like one day to return. Is it possible for me to return?"

"Yes, Davitch. Before you go; I will show you the way. I will show you how it is that you may return to us."

"It is the only promise I will make to you. I do not know what the Great Ocean has in store for us. I only know that we love you. I only know that we will always love you and that you will always find a home here with us."

"When you return to the world of men; you may take Sallon's keys with you. They cannot be lost nor stolen from you. They have become a part of you. The only way they can be taken from you is if you surrender them."

"They were his gift to you. They will be your way back to us."

"I will show you what lies in the Sanctuary and how to summon us there if you ever decide that you would return to us one day. If you decide to leave the world of men; you must first make it to that place. We will answer the Call and seek you there."

"Davitch. May I ask a question of you? You needn't answer me. But you must know that I love you as a child. I have loved you from the moment I first met you adrift on the ocean. I loved you for what you tried to do the day my sister's life was taken from her."

"Yes, Eden. You may ask me any question and if the answer lies within me, I will share it with you."

"Davitch; what third of Dolphin am I to be?"

"You are to be the same third of dolphin as Ebron and Neva. You are to be the same third of Dolphin as I. Eden; we are all of us to be of the same third. We are all of us to be pioneers in a new world after the coming of the shift."

"When the shift takes place; your people will make their presence known once again. It will be like a homecoming for you. All the crimes your people believe they committed will have been forgiven in the light of the beauty of the creatures you have become in this place."

"It is indeed a wonderful time to be alive."

"But the darkness still has much work to do before the shift occurs."

"We need only to survive until that time."

"We need only to love as deeply as we love and hope as deeply as we hope to know that that day will one day come. It is as certain as the sunrise. There can be no secrets among us, Eden."

"The shift is coming and there is nothing that man or dolphin can do to stop it. Do not be afraid."

We crossed the triangle and returned to the island. Night was falling when we entered the lagoon. We had been gone from this place for almost five moons.

We stood naked upon the beach once more.

Davitch wore a scar across his left breast ragged above his nipple as a reminder of his loss of his betrothed Tesla and their unborn son. He reached up and touched it as the tears fell from his face.

I knew that he would be leaving us soon. But for now there were things he needed to learn in anticipation of his one day returning to us.

Neva opened a pathway into the jungle canopy much like Tesla had done before her. Ebron and Davitch walked together as I followed closely behind to the clearing. The familiar rumbling beneath our feet signaled the rising dais. Neva opened the north portal and we all followed her down the stairwell into the light.

Ebron disappeared into one of the many rooms and returned with robes and sandals.

Neva had activated a device recessed into one the granite alcoves and produced a plate heaped with steaming rice and fish. We joined each other at a table lowered from an opposing wall and sat on chairs made from some light silvery metal which folded down from it.

We would be here for several days and there was much to learn; or rather there was much to teach; before we would depart this place again. We ate in silence; picking succulent pieces of fresh steaming fish and rice from the plate with our fingers and smiling at one another.

Neva once again retreated to the alcove and returned with a bowl of fruit that seemed to have been freshly picked from the lush tropical gardens above our heads. It was our dessert. After we finished we left into a stairwell that led us to a room which opened into a smaller hall.

With a wave of Neva's braceleted wrists, one of the walls became illuminated. Depicted on the wall was a three dimensional map of the planet as it existed many thousands of years ago. Eden's civilization had been extensive and reached every point on the compass. She waved her wrist again and most of her civilization disappeared off the map. Many parts of it were under thousands of feet of water.

The magnetic poles of the planet appeared to have shifted.

Also depicted on the map were the hundreds of intersects where man or dolphin could go to access universal power centers. Many of these centers have fallen into ruin or shifted to other places; some were submerged during the deluge; but some still exist today but are unrecognized for what they truly represent.

Eden pointed some of them out for me.

"Note the one's on your continent." she said. "Pay attention to the fluctuations in these intersects. You will be able to easily feel them; but others of your species are not aware enough to sense them."

"Tesla was correct. The human race does not see the elephant slowly walking to the watering hole."

"By paying attention, Davitch; You will know when he is about to roll. We have given you many gifts that you will discover as you grow older. Use them wisely."

Eden waved her wrist, and the map changed to the world as it exists today. It depicted the sprawl of the human species across the face of the globe.

She waved her wrist again.

"This is what the world will look like after the shift."

"Many of your species will survive."

"Many; however; will not."

"The elephant will not be allowed to perish."

"The flies on the other hand; have become a problem that threatens the survival of the elephant. Nature will not permit a fly to kill an elephant."

"If you should one day wish to depart your species and rejoin us in this place; it is my promise to you that you need only come here and wait. We will find you here."

"Come; there is many other things to show you." she said.

Eden led us out of the map room and into a hallway which followed down deeper into the granite below the great hall.

We entered into a warmly lit section of alcoves which circled above a theater of sorts below. We walked along the alcoves for a short distance until we came to a stairwell which led down into the well of the theater.

She led us to a wall of coral, and touched her bracelet to the circle of gold on the door and watched as it swung gently open. We stepped inside and watched as Eden walked up to a circular stone indentation filled with water.

"This is how you will find us Davitch" she said.

Eden took her finger and dipped it into the water. She smiled and soon ripples began to vibrate away from her finger, slowly at first; one small ripple at a time. Then the ripples began to grow larger. She wasn't moving her finger at all. She was just standing there smiling.

"This is all you will need to do. Put you finger in the water and think of us. When the ripple becomes a wave and washes over the edge of this cistern; you will have called us here. You can be absolutely certain that we have heard your call."

"Now, to the library. I know how much you love to read. So I am going to loan you a book. You may keep this book as long as you like on one condition." she said.

As she continued speaking we made our way out of the room and across the floor of the theater to yet another room. Again, one small touch of her wrist to the door and it swung open inward.

"This book will teach you our language. It is a primer that will teach you where we came from; who we are; why we came here and many, many, other things."

"Would you like to read it? Do you wish to take it with you?"

I looked at Eden. She was holding a book that appeared to be many hundreds and hundreds of pages thick. Perhaps thousands of pages thick. It appeared to be bound in gold. My first thought was, "How am I supposed to carry it?"

She smiled and laughed and her eyes sparkled.

"We owe you this much for having loved us as you do."

"You must only promise to return it to us one day. But the only way you can return it..is by returning..."

"Yes, of course, Eden. But..But...how am I supposed to....?"

"Carry it?"

"Yes?"

"Like this."

She pointed to a divan in the center of the library and said "Lie down and watch."

She reached into the thick front cover of the book and pulled out an ornate circular band of gold that was recessed into it.

"Put this on and close your eyes. It won't hurt and it will only take a moment."

I did as she instructed. I felt the cool metal softly melt against my forehead and then suddenly my mind exploded with brilliant images flashing like lightning; thousands upon thousands of images and symbols and faces and scenes flooding into my mind. For a brief moment I thought my head would explode; but I could hear Eden in my mind saying "You're mind has plenty of room for it all. Take it and read it later."

She was right. It only took a few moments. I could feel her hands taking the circle of gold from my forehead and helping me up to a sitting position.

I was laughing.

"Was that fun? Davitch."

All I could think of saying was "I can read, Mom.... Eden....I can read."

"No little boy. You can do more than that."

"We know that you will return to us one day."

"We know also that you will leave us soon."

"We are at peace with that."

"Your coming was a great joy to us and your parting will be a great sorrow. But knowing that you will one day return to us is our peace in this."

"You will come back Davitch? You will come back, one day??"

"Yes, Eden. I promise I will come back."

We left the sanctuary after resting and grieving for several days. Over the course of those several days Eden gave me many more books to "read." We left everything as we had found it; and departed the island for the coastal waters of the southern shores.

There were other things we wished to show Davitch before we let him go. We sensed his heart was torn.

He had lost Tesla. There was nothing left for him to return to in the world of men. He had spoken of a younger brother lost somewhere out there. He had barely begun to explore his world when he was thrown from it.

We had no right to keep him from it. But we had no right to keep him in ours.

We could see him looking toward it with greater frequency. We knew it would not be long before we parted company. Ebron and Neva spoke to me silently about how to make that parting easier on him.

We knew the moment he stood upon dry land again he would be as we had first found him; naked; and without any resources to make his way in the world of men. But we knew too; that he had been given gifts that he could use to ease his way if he chose.

In the world of humans, in the minds of men; he had become a giant among them. He would do well to conceal those gifts. Or he would become a target soon enough.

We had made our way into the archipelago of islands that wend slowly westward. Davitch expressed a small familiarity with these islands.

He called them the Keys.

It was there where we decided it was best that we parted ways.

Our parting with Davitch is a private thing. Dolphins weep. In their hearts they grieve as humans do. We stood high in the water in the falling light of that sunset and waved our farewell to the boy standing alone on the deserted beach. We turned on our tails; and leapt silently into the night. We love you and we will miss you.

We will meet again, Davitch. As the Great Ocean is our witness. We will meet again.

Chapter Fifteen

"I am compromise. A little muck. A bargain struck. Down on luck."
"I will become a compromise. A bad idea. A rape. A vicious fuck."

We were somewhere off the Florida Keys with a dead bloating corpse stinking up one of the crew cabins. The order was given to make for the closest port. Any port. The nearest one was Key West.

We were diverting to Key West. After just two days at sea; we were heading into port.

Key West was the toilet bowl of America. Every time America flushed; some turd swirled around the bowl and ended up bobbing aimlessly at the end of the road. The end of the road just happened to be at the southern most point in the continental United States. The proverbial end of the road.

Every kind of hairball; screwball; dirt ball; or scum ball that America could flush down its sewer pipe was here. Of course; that was before the days of the cruise ships and t-shirt shops.

We arrived just before sunset and landed at Mallory Square.

There was a small problem with that.

The Rita was 700 foot long. Mallory Square was the only wharf in Key West long enough to accommodate her. Mallory Square on the other hand; was the only place that could accommodate the hundreds of sun worshipers who gathered every night to watch the sun go down.

It was a time honored tradition. The hippies; druggies; drunks; wackos; weirdos; street performers; pickpockets; pimps; hookers; hustlers; addicts and assholes all had a bet on the exact moment when the sun would peel away from the horizon and drop unexpectedly from sight.

When that awe inspiring event occurred; which it has been doing now for say; about 4 billion years or so on a pretty regular basis; they would all start clapping. The clapping would signal the beginning of what would then turn into a free for all block party the like of which Key West was infamously famous for.

Boy did we piss them off.

A crowd had already begun to gather to watch the daily ritual of the sunset.

What were we supposed to do?

Put the dead bloating body in the walk in freezer? Bury the guy at sea? That only happens in the movies.

It was the beginning of a seven day party.

Everybody was already stoned when the ship creased into the side of the pilings of Mallory Square. Here comes this huge rust bucket of a ship just in time to block everybody's perfect view of the sunset.

The Captain had radioed ahead and the Coast Guard had sent a detachment down to catch lines. There was no tug boat to push us in so we used winches. We snapped two three inch trying to pull the ship into the niggerheads on the pier.

Old Willy Eubanks was yelling his head off trying to get the gawkers to stand clear. It's a wonder to me that nobody was cut in half when those lines let go.

They whine like a dog before they snap.

Everybody was crowding around when Riley lowered the gang plank over the rail. They all wanted to see what was going on. When we carried the body off the ship they made way. You could smell the stench from a hundred yards if the breeze was right.

The Conch Salad Man didn't make much that night. The smell just seemed to linger in the air.

Of course there was an investigation. Why wasn't the man on the ship's manifest? Good question. Was he an illegal? Good question. Did somebody kill him? Good question. And on and on and on.

But I was an American. I didn't have to wait for Customs and Immigration to clear me. I was free to come and go as I pleased. We were back on port shift. Eight hours on during the day and the rest of the time off.

This was where I really found out how things worked.

Willy wanted me to find him a woman. He didn't care if she was fat or skinny; young or old; black or white. He wanted a woman. Plain and simple. So I suppose that made me a pimp. Here I was in my first foreign country. Key West was about as foreign a country back then as you could get; and looking for a woman for the First Mate of the ship I was a crew member of.

I was so far removed from where I had come from it might has well have been the moon.

Willy gave me a hundred bucks and told me to find him some cooze. That's what he called it.

For those seven days; I became an errand boy in the bizarre world of Key West, Florida. It was an adventure the likes of which few can compare.

In many ways those seven days in Key West were a harbinger of what was to come for me. My life had become a study in extremes. I could write a book just about those seven days. I wasn't off the ship a half an hour before I managed to score some weed. It was everywhere. Finding a woman for Willy took a few hours longer.

I don't remember her name. I just remember that she was young. Early twenty's maybe. I don't really remember. But I remember she looked like she fell out of the ugly tree and hit every branch on the way down. I guess that kind of made me a pimp; huh?

Willy didn't care; he just wanted a warm body to hold.

Key West was where I really got to know William Eubanks. I was the most convenient errand boy he had ever know. I was thorough and reliable. When he wanted something; he called for me. I didn't get much sleep while I was there.

Key West was where I was introduced to the concept of "make work."

That's where we would take a small patch of the rusting hulk and paint it. It gave us something to do while we were doing nothing. We were waiting while everybody figured out what happened to the dead assistant cook. We weren't going anywhere until the authorities were satisfied and their investigation was complete.

Those seven days were a blur. But I made a friend in Willy Eubanks.

When we sailed from Key West seven days later, everyone clapped to see us go. We had blocked their view of the sunset for a full week.

We made Progresso about ten days later. We picked the dolphins up just off the Dry Tortugas and they followed us into and all the way across the Gulf of Mexico.

A pilot came on Board in Progresso and took us up the coast of the Yucatan. We were in Ancient Mayan coastal waters and still the same pod of dolphins followed us.

They had been with us for over two weeks. It was strange.

When we got to this tiny little place called Los Colorados; the Captain radioed for a Tugboat to bring us in. He had never been to Los Colorados. Nobody on board except the pilot had been here before. I was on watch in the wheelhouse.

I remember the Pilot shaking his head. " No tugboat. No tugboat." The Captain looked at him like "What do you mean? No tug?"

Everybody busted out laughing when this old guy in a rowboat came rowing out with a towline to pull in the hawsers. We had to winch our way in. No tugboats here, boss. Just old guys with row boats and road salt.

The town was a striking example of poverty in slow motion. If you ever wonder where they get the road salt they sell in the little bags at Walmart; don't. They make it here. If you wonder where they get the salt they spread on the roads in the winter; don't. They make it here in little coastal towns like these. Sure, some salt is mined, but most of it comes from places like Los Colorados.

Western society rides on the shoulders of little towns like these. Western society rides on the undeveloped backs of third world countries in little faraway places like this.

It was like stepping into another dimension.

Road salt. Something as simple as road salt.

I was amazed.

The whole town worked the salt fields.

They had tidal flood gates that they would open allowing the sea to flood enormous plains that they had excavated. They would close the gates and over a relatively short period of time nature would do the work for them. Evaporation would slowly remove the moisture leaving behind enormous beds of sea salt. The salt would be bulldozed into piles, loaded onto ships like ours and exported to countries to be spread on sidewalks; road; bridges; whatever.

Andre and I opened shop while we were there. There were no women to be had. The town had less than a thousand residents. It had an open air theater that showed black and white movies with Spanish sub-titles on an old reel to reel projector. No one had a vehicle. Everybody walked or rode rickety bicycles. The salt company owned everything.

The open air bar was straight out of a Pancho Villa movie. The only thing missing was a Mexican sleeping on the stoop in a huge sombrero.

Andre struck on the idea first. We spent a couple of hours going through the rag bins in the engine room until we had a sizable bundle of good used clothing. Our first night in Los Colorados was spent in barter with the locals; with Andre exacting almost ridiculously cruel prices for what were to us nothing more than rags.

By the end of the night; we had more cold Mexican beer than we could possibly drink; so we sold it on promise to some of the other men on the ship. When payday came we would get our pay as well as some of the other men's pay.

We had company wherever we went. Children mostly. No one was hungry here. They were just poor. Dirt poor.

I was falling deeper into the world. This was part of my education. Can you spell poverty? Of course you can. There is a certain callous that develops on your eyes the more you see of it.

It took two days to load the ship with salt. We were going to take it to Vera Cruz.

When we left Los Colorados; I never looked back.

Hanz started shooting at the dolphins shortly after breakfast on the morning that we left.

It was that morning he shot and killed Mara. That was the morning of my death or birth, depending on how you look at it. I wonder what they ever figured out would be their story about what happened to me? The kid? He must have committed suicide.

Maybe I should have thrown Hanz overboard instead of the Enfield. No... I got the better end of it all. And Eden...someday Eden...someday....I will ask you if you did. Because now you and I are both authors of this Orphan Creed, and hidden in it's words are indeed the pathways home.

Epilogue

"Davitch, I will be here. Waiting. I am under the same sky as you. When you tire of the world of men, will you come back to us?"

"Yes Eden, and I will be bringing a guest with me. I just don't know who it is yet. But I promise I will come. Upon the shift will I see you again."

In the falling light, the naked boy turned from the ocean and walked from the sand of the beach back into the world of men, still orphaned, but not alone. As his form began to disappear into the tropic foliage, the fading light glimmered brilliantly on two golden bracelets that seemed to be slowly melting into his wrists, leaving only footprints in the sand to mark his even passing by.....

The End of the
Beginning